The Mystery

of

Craven Manor

Joy Wodhams

Also by Joy Wodhams

ADULT AND YOUNG ADULT NOVELS
Me, Dingo And Sibelus
The Girl In The Attic
Affair With An Angel
The Reluctant Bride
Never Sleep With A Neighbour!
Cabbage Boy
SHORT STORY COLLECTIONS
The Floater
The Girl At Table Nine
NOVELS FOR CHILDREN
There's A Lion In My Bed
The Boy Who Could Fly
The Family On Pineapple Island
CREATIVE WRITING
How To Write Fiction

Joy Wodhams has been writing as long as she can remember. She is the descendant of five generations of theatre and circus gymnasts, trapeze artists, singers, musicians and songwriters. As far as she is aware she is the first fiction writer in the family.

1

The Runaway

The truck driver who'd dropped Matt at the crossroads had told him the station was only five minutes walk but he couldn't find it. He couldn't even find the railway line and he'd been searching for more than an hour.

Now it was raining. Huge heavy drops that dive bombed the back of his neck. And his trainers were letting in water. They squelched with every step.

He wondered what else could go wrong. He thought he'd planned every last detail but here he was, only three hours from the Home, and he had no idea where he was. To add to his misery he'd lost his phone somewhere along the way.

He shivered, staring out at the sodden landscape, empty except for a couple of crows blowing like black rags across the darkening sky. He was scared. Maybe he should give up, go back to that last house he'd seen more than half a mile back and ask the owners for help. But what if they asked questions? Called the police?

On the horizon he could see woodland. He'd be drier there, might even be able to sleep, as long as he didn't think about all the creepies that came out at night. Snakes, bugs, bats – things that hunted and killed in the shadows. Not that he was afraid of stuff like that, he told himself.

For a moment he wished he was back at the Home, sitting at the big kitchen table with the others, tucking into whatever Mrs Doherty had cooked for their dinner. It was Wednesday. Wednesday was usually meat pie and mash.

If he hadn't worked himself into such a state, he could be there now. Instead of which, here he stood, cold, soaked to the skin, alone and completely lost.

There was no way back. Pulling up his collar he sprinted for the distant line of trees.

The rain grew heavier. He sneezed, a sudden explosion of sound that brought a flutter of complaint from a roosting bird somewhere nearby. That's all I need, he thought. A cold! Wrapping his jacket more closely around him he lay down and curled himself into a tight damp ball. He coughed experimentally. And sneezed again. By morning, he decided gloomily, he would probably have pneumonia. Maybe Dad would be sorry then.

Tears filled his eyes, real tears, and he sat up and scrubbed at them furiously.

"I'm not crying!" he said, glaring out into the blackness, "I'm not! I'm not!".

2

Tramp

In his dream he was scrambling over rocks towards a sea that broke on the shore in a froth of green and silver. He flung himself at the waves, gasping at their coldness, not really bothering to swim but letting himself be tossed back and forth like a stray cork in the tide. The air filled his lungs like sharp clear menthol and he let out a shout of sheer pleasure. Then his Dad was calling him for breakfast, Mum was smiling down from the top of the cliff, and there was a smell of something frying

"Well, mate, are you going to wake up? Or do I have to eat it all on me own?"

Matt opened his eyes. The dream faded.

"Don't you want any? I always say meself there ain't nothing like bangers for breakfast."

The speaker leaned forward and poked at a blackened frying pan that rested on a small fire of twigs, then squatted back on his haunches and regarded Matt from clear blue eyes that appeared much younger than the rest of him. His hair was long, white and matted, his beard streaked dull yellow. He looked like an unkempt polar bear.

A rich smell rose from the spluttering sausages and Matt licked his lips. He was hungry and the food, hot food, drew him. His clothes, still damp from a night's exposure, clung to him as he sat up.

He watched as the tramp delved into various hidden openings amongst his clothing – a many-layered collection of coats, blankets and even what appeared to be a rag rug, all held together with pins and string – and produced a plastic plate and a tin lid, half a loaf, grubby at the corners, and a penknife. Transferring the sausages from the frying pan to the dishes, he hacked off two thick slices of bread and threw them into the pan to mop up the fat.

"You can have the plate," he told Matt. "Seeing you're the guest."

From elsewhere in his wardrobe he plucked a tin with a wire handle, a screw topped jar containing tea and another of sugar and two paper cups, the sort that pop out of vending machines, which he stood on a stone away from the fire. A plastic lemonade bottle filled with water rested by his feet and this he emptied into the tin, together with a handful of tea and another of sugar. A quick stir with his knife and then he balanced the tin carefully on the fire to boil.

"I always say there ain't nothing like a nice brew of tea to set you going," he said. "Now then, eat up, mate. Get your teeth into it."

"What about forks?" asked Matt.

"Forks? Blimey, what d'you think I am? A walking Debenhams? Use yer fingers, mate."

Matt stared at his plate. He was hungry and the blackened fat from the frying pan disguised the dirt on the edges of the bread. Gingerly he picked up one of the sausages and took a bite. It was delicious. Within five minutes his plate was clean. The tea, stewed as it was and the colour of treacle, tasted marvellous in the fresh morning air.

Afterwards the tramp scrubbed his beard with the end of his sleeve and gave a belch of satisfaction.

"There, mate, not even the top chef at the Savoy could've done better than that. Yes, I'm a good cook," he said complacently.

"Have you always been a tramp?" asked Matt.

"Tramp? *Tramp?* Gentleman of the road, that's me. I've been travelling the roads for – oh – must be near fifty years. 'Alf a century. There ain't much I couldn't tell you about being on the road. Why, I could write a book about it. One of them books you see in shop windows. Self-survival, that's the thing. 'Ow to find food - 'Ow to tell the weather - 'Ow to sleep warm at night. Yes, I've a good mind to do that one of these days. Write a best seller. Have a Rolls Royce and caviar for supper and a pretty woman to wait on me." He grinned, showing stained but strong teeth. "Yes, I might just do that."

"But what were you before?" asked Matt. "Before you became a – a gentleman of the road?"

The tramp pondered. "Oh, this and that. Odd jobs. Went to sea till I got drunk and missed me ship. Took a job in a factory then." He shook his head. "Didn't like that. Shut in all day and all that noise. No, the road's best."

He rummaged among his clothes, producing a flat tin of tobacco and a packet of cigarette papers. Carefully he shook a few strands of the tobacco into a paper, rolled it between his fingers, licked the end and stuck the thin crumpled cylinder between his lips. It flared dangerously as he lit it. Belatedly he offered the tin to Matt. "Want one?"

Matt shook his head quickly. "No thanks."

"That's right," nodded the tramp. "Nothing worse for your health," he said and coughed to prove it. "One of these days I'll give 'em up meself, just like that. Throw the tin away and never 'ave another one."

He lapsed into silence and Matt watched the end of the cigarette glow spasmodically as the old man puffed. Specks of burning paper drifted into the air.

"You've run off, 'aven't you?"

Matt looked away from the tramp's shrewd eyes.

"Stands to reason you wouldn't be sleeping out for fun," the tramp explained. "Not a lad like you, not without a tent you wouldn't, and a sleeping bag and one of them Primus things. No," he said, staring at Matt speculatively, "I reckon you're on the run, me lad."

Matt licked his lips but said nothing.

"Now which is it, I wonder? Mum and Dad? Police? An 'Ome?" The tramp gave Matt a reassuring smile. "You don't 'ave to worry about me, you know. I'll not send you back."

"Home," Matt mumbled.

"Ah." The tramp nodded. "Was in one of them meself years ago. Did they beat you?"

"Beat me? No, of course not."

"They did me. Every week, near enough." The tramp's eyes hardened. "Too independent for them, you see. They didn't like that. Nor me running away 'alf the time. Nasty things, 'Omes." He took the ragged end of the cigarette from his mouth, examined it with regret and stubbed it out on a flat stone. "Still, I expect they're different nowadays. I don't suppose the Welfare will let 'em rough you up like they used to."

"They wouldn't anyway." Matt found himself jumping to the defence of the Home. He wasn't going to have anyone saying bad things about Mrs Doherty and Mr Garner. The others – some of the older boys who took such delight in picking on him, messing up his clothes, hiding his possessions, calling him Matilda because of his blonde hair and small stature – well, they were different. "It's just – not a real home," he finished.

"Well, I never 'ad one of them so I wouldn't know," said the tramp. He glanced up at the sky. "Nine o'clock, thereabouts. Time we got the washing up done."

The washing up was accomplished by swilling out the cups with the last inch of water from the bottle and wiping the tins and frying pan with a torn sheet of newspaper. Within seconds they had disappeared into their various hideyholes about the tramp's person and the rope that held everything together was being retied with a complicated series of knots.

"Well then," he said when he was finished. "I must be off."

"Where are you going?"

"Oh, this way, that way. Maybe towards Birmingham."

Matt stole a glance at the old man. He was dirty and smelly, but he had cooked him breakfast and he knew what he was doing and where he was going and he would be company. "Can I – can I come with you?" he asked.

The tramp paused. "Not a good idea, mate. No, not a good idea."

"Why not?"

"Don't like to be lumbered," the tramp said abruptly. "I'm used to travelling alone."

Matt sighed.

"Stand on your own two feet. Independence, that's the thing." The tramp stood up, scattered the dying fire with a mud-caked boot and began to move away.

Matt called after him. "Thanks for breakfast."

The tramp turned his head. "And thank *you*. Thank *you*." He gave Matt a strange little smile and strode off.

Matt watched until the old man disappeared from sight. It was only later after he had cleaned himself up and brushed down his clothes as best he could that he realised something else had disappeared.

His savings. The £50 that he had scraped together since Christmas was gone.

3

Matt Meets Samantha

Stand on your own two feet! Matt raged as he pushed his way through the trees, uncaring of the branches that caught and tore at his clothes. Be independent! If the tramp had believed in independence he wouldn't be stealing from others.

Matt had quite liked the old man, yet all the time he had chatted, cooked breakfast, shared his food, he had had Matt's money, the money that had taken so long to save and that he needed so badly if he was to survive on his own.

He must have stolen it while Matt was sleeping. Yet why hadn't he disappeared as soon as he got it? Was he so desperate for company that he had taken the risk of Matt noticing his loss? But what could Matt have done anyway? Called the police? Well, whatever the tramp's reasons he was now £50 better off and Matt was in a fix.

What could he do? He couldn't take a bus or train, he couldn't risk hitching any more rides. He wondered if he could disguise himself, find something to darken his blonde hair, rough his clothes up a bit and take to the road – maybe people would think he was just a gypsy kid from the nearest encampment – or he could give himself up to the police and be taken back to the Home. Matt scowled. No , he was not going back.

But from now on he wouldn't trust anyone. Nobody

was honest. Nobody cared. Well, he wouldn't care either.

He trudged on, pushing through hedges, climbing fences, instinctively avoiding the roads. The fields were sodden, and mud caked him below the knees. He met no-one. A few solitary cows noted his progress but the further he travelled the more alone he felt. And now the sole of his left trainer had split completely and, hell, it was raining again.

Ahead, beyond a barbed wire fence and two more fields, lay another mass of trees. He would make for it and hole up for a while.

The trees' canopy was dense enough to provide cover but Matt was already soaked, and his ruined trainers sucked up mud with every step. Listlessly he wandered through the trees, hardly caring which direction he took.

"You're trespassing. Don't you know these are private woods?"

He swung round, startled. Between the trees stood a large black horse. On its back sat a slender girl of about his own age.

"Well? Haven't you a tongue in your head?" The girl gave an exasperated sigh and swung herself to the ground. "What are you doing in our woods?" she demanded.

Matt stared into a pair of sharp blue eyes, level with his own and set in a small narrow face. A black riding hat was rammed down over red-gold eyebrows.

"*Your* woods?" he repeated.

"Yes, ours." The girl waved her crop. "All this belongs to Craven Manor. Didn't you read the signs?"

"No, I - "

"Never mind. What are you doing here?"

"I – I suppose I'm lost."

"You look as if you've been lost for a long time, you're in a bit of a mess, aren't you?" Her small sharp nose wrinkled in distaste. "And you smell like a camel!"

Matt sniffed. He would have described it as more of a wet dog smell. Half heartedly he tried to brush away the damp earth and mud that clung to his trousers.

"You'll never get it off like that," said the girl. "They need drying out and brushing with a clothes brush. Or better still, a good wash. You'd better come back with me." She measured him with her eyes. "A pair of my jeans should fit you. How old are you?"

"Eleven. Nearly twelve."

"I'm twelve already." The black horse ambled forward and nudged her gently, reminding her of its presence. "Do you ride?"

"Only bikes."

"Bikes!" she scoffed. "I've got two cups for riding. And sixteen rosettes. I've got medals for dancing too. Ballet." She struck a pose, ridiculous in her hacking jacket and jodhpurs.

Matt looked away. He had no time for conceited females. He had enough problems. "Look, I'm going. Sorry about your woods and all that, but I don't think I've done any damage."

"No, wait! Where do you live?"

"Oh, over that way," he indicated vaguely.

"No you don't. Nobody lives that way except the Farleys, and you're certainly not one of them. So where have you come from?"

"It's none of your business, is it?" he snapped.

She stared at him. "Are you a gypsy?"

"Maybe."

"You don't talk like one."

Matt shrugged and turned away.

"Wait!"

He sighed. Just my luck, he thought, being caught by the owners of these woods – or at least, by their snooty daughter. Well, if she thinks she can order me about she's mistaken. I'm going.

But he had barely taken half a dozen steps when her clear voice reached him again.

"Now I know who you are. You're that boy on the local radio – the one that's missing from a Home. You are, aren't you?" The girl jumped up and down. "I'm right, aren't I? What fun! Oh, don't worry, I shan't tell anyone, I promise. In fact – in fact, I'll help you – if you'll help me."

"Help *you*? How?"

She paused. "I don't know yet. But I'll think of something. What's your name? Matthew something, isn't it?"

He was reluctant to give her his full name, but he supposed everyone who listened to the radio had heard it by now. "Bright. Matthew Bright."

"Mine's Samantha Cooper. You can call me Sam if you like." She leaned closer, her face sharpening with curiosity. "Tell me all about it. Why did you run away?"

He saw no reason to explain to this arrogant girl with her posh accent and bossy manner. "Oh, well, you know what orphanages and homes are like. Beatings and everything …."

"Really?" Her eyes brightened. "Tell me some

more!"

"I'd rather not talk about it if you don't mind. It was all a bit -" He sighed. "Harrowing."

"Goodness," she breathed. "So what are you going to do? Where will you go?"

"I don't know. At the moment I haven't any money." He told her about the tramp.

She nodded. "People are rotten."

"You're telling me!"

"You can't do anything without money," she said. "You can't get a train or a bus. You can't get a taxi. And if you hitchhike someone might guess who you are, like I did."

"I know all that! But whatever happens, I'm not going back."

"Well then, we'd better get you into hiding."

She sprang up and remounted her horse.

"Come on," she urged. "Climb up behind me."

He shook his head. "No fear!"

"Scared?" she taunted.

"Of course not. I just don't think it's a good idea to come to your house. What about your parents? If you know who I am, they probably will too."

"My parents aren't there."

"Are they due back soon?"

"No. They're – they're not due back at all."

"You mean - ?" What *did* she mean? "Are they dead?" he asked carefully.

"Dead? Of course they're not dead, *stupid!* Why should they be dead?"

He stared at her, watching her pale face screw up and redden with fury. "For heaven's sake, I was only asking!"

"Well, they're not dead. They're just not there. They – if you must know, they've been kidnapped."

"Ah. I see."

She looked at him sharply. "You don't believe me, do you? You're like everyone else. Nobody believes me."

"Of course I believe you if you say so," said Matt. But he didn't. There were kids at the Home who told tales about their parents. Kenny Green's parents had been snatched by Martians. Marian Phillips' mother was not really dead, she was a famous film star in Hollywood. Tony Ricconi's father was in the Mafia and had hidden Tony at the Home so that a rival gang wouldn't capture him. It was all make-believe. It made them feel more important, made them feel better. He wondered why Sam needed to feel better.

"So …. Who's actually looking after you?"

Her mouth tightened. "Nobody."

"Somebody has to. You can't live on your own."

"Oh, there are people around but they're not – they don't – they're just there. Anyway, they weren't listening to the local radio last night, they were far too busy having one of their meetings – and I can easily think up a story to explain why you're here."

She jerked the reins and the horse pranced sideways. "Come on, I want my lunch."

So did Matt. But he still hung back. Did he really want to get involved with this crazy girl? And what had she meant about helping her? He couldn't even help himself! And if the people at this Craven Manor suspected who he was they would certainly call the police. No, he was safer on his own.

"Thanks, but I think it's too risky."

"I'll tell them you're someone else – a friend from school or something. Don't worry, I'm good at lying. Anyway, they won't tell the police, honestly they won't. They don't want anything to do with the police." Her voice cracked with appeal. "Please come."

Matt fidgeted. He *was* hungry. Starving, in spite of the tramp's breakfast. And he *did* need some dry clothes. Sam's offer was tempting , and perhaps he'd be able to slip away after lunch.

"I can lend you some money. For the train or whatever."

He looked up at her. "Why would you?"

She shrugged. "Why not? I've got plenty."

He believed her. But could he trust her? Why was she keen to take him home with her? And what had she meant when she said he could help *her?*

Well, beggars couldn't be choosers, and what other options did he have? "All right, I'll come."

"Great!" Sam leaned down, grabbed his hand and heaved. In one clumsy scramble Matt found himself mounted behind her. Indignant at its double burden, the horse reared, almost shooting him straight off again and then they were away, plunging madly through the trees.

"Hey, slow down!" Matt yelled, then wished he hadn't, for Sam as if challenged dug her heels into the horse's flanks and galloped faster than before.

"You're mad!" he shouted.

In reply she sawed on the reins, causing the horse to rear again and Matt to slide yet closer to the horse's tail, then set off once more at the same headlong pace.

"Stop! I want to get down! NOW!"

"Get down?" she repeated. With a high, almost hysterical laugh she lashed out with her crop, stripping the branches about her of their leaves and on they plunged through a blinding falling storm of green.

Matt gave up. Locking his arms tightly around his crazy companion, he screwed his eyes shut and prayed.

The terrifying ride ended at last.

"Better than a *bicycle*, isn't it?" Sam shouted. "*Now* you can get down."

Matt opened his eyes and released his grip. His descent to the ground was painful. He felt as if all the bones in his body had been ground down and reshaped and none of them fitted together any more. Taking a few wobbling steps away from the horse, he stared up at the blank walls that confronted him.

They were high. At least three and a half metres high, cemented smooth as marble. Jagged shards of glass were fixed on edge along the top. Two enormous wooden gates, bound with iron, formed a forbidding entrance. It looked like a prison.

Sam pressed a button set in a box beside the gates.

"Who is there?" came a hollow mechanical voice from the box.

She snorted with impatience. "It's me. Who else?" There followed a long pause and then slowly the gates opened.

"Wait! Where are we?"

"Why, my home, of course. Craven Manor."

Sam took up the reins and began to lead the horse up the drive, but paused before they had gone more than a few steps.

"Don't say anything about the kidnapping, will you?"

There was no risk of that!

She looked at him and her eyes were bleak.

"It's all true you know. What I said. And some day I'll prove it!"

4

Craven Manor

The grounds were magnificent but an air of neglect hung over everything. Hedges went untrimmed, dandelions grew in the gravel of the broad drive, the lawns had lost their velvet smoothness. Someone had started to mow them and given up half way through. A ride-on mower stood abandoned near a bed of straggly roses.

The house stood grey and square at the end of the drive. As they crunched towards it Matt counted twenty two windows. Good grief, it was even bigger than the Home.

"Is this really your house?" he asked Sam.

"Yes, of course. Although Daddy kept – Daddy keeps threatening to sell it. He says no-one but a fool would live in it, 'cos it costs a fortune to heat and architecturally he says it's a dreadful hotchpotch. The middle bit's Tudor and the sides are Georgian and there's a Victorian annexe at the back. But I don't think he'd ever really give it up. We've lived here for three hundred years, you see."

Three hundred years. Matt tried to imagine it.

They turned into a yard at the rear of the house and Sam stabled the horse, rubbed him down and gave him water.

"Come on, let's get lunch." She was running towards the house.

"Wait!" Matt called. He looked back at the huge gates and the high walls that surrounded the house. "Look, I don't like this. Are you sure it's ok to have me here?"

"Sure I'm sure."

Matt wished he had her confidence.

After the pale brilliance of outdoors the entrance hall was a dim cave Only gradually did Matt become aware of the carved staircase and polished oak floor, the darkly timbered walls and the huge gilt framed portraits that hung row above row. Sunshine struggled through leaded windows and glimmered here and there on pale narrow faces with painted eyes that followed him wherever he moved.

"D'you like it?"

"Spooky! I mean, all those people staring at you. And so dark. It must be really scary at night."

She was affronted. "It's not scary at all. And they're not just people, they're my relatives. That's my great great grandfather, George Ferris Cooper." She pointed to a black garbed gentleman with a forbidding square-bearded face. "And that's his great great grandfather, Simon Ferris Cooper," she added, indicating another in pale grey satin and lace. "And that's Alice Sarah Cooper, my great grandmother, and that's her sister Adelaide, and that's my uncle -"

"Oh, all right, you don't have to go on and on!" Matt felt a wave of irritation wash over him.

"Well, of course, if you're not interested …."

"No, I'm not!"

She gave him a patronising look that contained a touch of cruelty. "I suppose I shouldn't expect someone from a Home to appreciate background. After all, if you haven't a proper family yourself you can't have any idea what it's like to have ancestors stretching back hundreds of years."

"Everybody has ancestors, and mine stretch back just as far as yours. Anyway, they're all dead now so what does it matter? And everybody has a family. My mother's dead but I've still got a father."

"So why are you in a Home?"

"He's looking for a better job and then he's going to buy a house by the sea. We're going to live there together, just the two of us - " Matt's voice trailed away. I'm doing just what the other kids do, he told himself. Make believe, all make believe.

She stared at him for a moment. Then she turned and led the way across the hall to a narrow door. "Come on, I'm starving."

Her feet in their polished brown boots clattered on the stone flagged passage to the kitchen. Matt in his damp ragged trainers padded softly behind her. He wished he could have cleaned himself up before meeting anyone else.

The kitchen, almost as large as the hall, was lighter and brighter. A fire burned in the inglenook fireplace and copper pans and flowered china decorated the open shelves that rose above pine cupboards. It was a welcoming room, but ash from the fire spilled forward on the hearth, leaving a white bloom over every surface, the brass fender was tarnished and the modern stainless steel cooker that stood next to the old black range was spotted with grease. Used crockery was stacked carelessly in the sink.

At a table in the centre of the room a woman lounged behind an open newspaper. Somehow, Matt thought, she looked out of place in the old fashioned country kitchen. That tight low-cut dress, scarlet with white spots, the make-up, glistening red lips and turquoise eye shadow, and the strappy shoes with heels that were at least six inches high. She looked more like Tracey, one of the helpers at the Home, when she was dressed to go out clubbing.

"Irene, we want lunch."

"We? Who's we?" The newspaper was lowered. The woman stared at Matt, eyes narrowed. "Who's your friend?"

"Just a friend," said Sam. "From my school."

"Do *they* know he's here?" Irene jerked elaborate blonde curls at the ceiling.

"Not yet."

"They won't like it."

Sam glared at Irene. "Who cares?"

More and more uneasy, Matt backed towards the door. "Perhaps I'd better not stay," he said.

"You're staying," Sam ordered. "Come on, Irene, we want lunch."

Irene yawned and turned the page of her paper. "I'm not making lunch yet. It's only eleven thirty."

"If you don't," said Sam, "I'll tell *her* about the money you pinched from her handbag." She parked herself on the end of the table and began to hum a little tune. "And *she* won't like that!"

"Well, well! Proper little madam, aren't you?" Irene

smiled a small cold smile but she put the paper aside and rose to fill a kettle.

Sam winked at Matt and swung down from the table. "Sausages," she commanded, "and bacon and eggs."

"I don't like eggs," said Matt.

"Bacon and eggs," she continued as if he had not spoken. "And ice cream and coffee."

Was it worth mentioning that he would rather have tea or a Coke, he wondered? No.

"And we'll have it in the conservatory," ended Sam triumphantly.

Matt had never seen anything like it. It rose two storeys high to a domed stained glass roof, below which giant tropical plants twined, twisted or hung like ropes from creeper-covered beams. They grew so rampantly that little light penetrated the glass walls, but an occasional shaft of sunlight pierced the domed roof to cast jewel coloured shadows on the jungle below. Somewhere there was a faint tinkle of water. The air was humid. Matt wiped his brow.

"Well?" asked Sam.

"It's – it's very nice."

"*Very nice!*" exploded Sam. "Do you know people have come from far and wide to see this conservatory? There are plants here from all over Africa and South America. There are plants that even Kew Gardens haven't got! My father's collection is one of the best in the world. *Very nice!*" she repeated scornfully.

Matt pulled his tee shirt away from his chest. He guessed the temperature must be about 40 degrees. Surely people didn't normally eat in here. "Don't you think it's a bit hot?"

"No! I think it's just right. Anyway, the plants need it."

"Well, I don't know much about plants."

"Obviously not! Here, come and look at this one." She led him to a tall plant that sported pairs of tooth-edged protruberances like open mouths on the ends of its leaves. "Now watch." She picked up a dead fly from the corner of a window frame and dropped it carefully on to one of the mouths. Instantly the jaws snapped together on the fly.

"There," she said. "I bet you've never seen a carnivorous plant before. Would you like to feed it?"

"No thanks!"

"But don't you think it's interesting?"

"I think it's pretty gruesome if you want to know."

She gave a contemptuous snort. "The trouble with you is you've no education. You just can't appreciate anything that's different."

"And the trouble with you is you think anyone that disagrees with you is stupid!"

They were arguing again, unaware that Irene had entered and was regarding them with cool amusement. She carried a heavily laden tray towards a curly-legged iron table and set it down with a loud crash, slopping coffee over the tops of the cups. She raised a pencilled eyebrow at Sam.

"I hope there's no complaints."

Sam stared at her coolly. "I'll soon let you know if there are."

When Irene had gone Matt stared at the plates of fried food. His appetite had gone. It must be the heat, he decided, and that business with the plant. He poked his fork half heartedly into the egg and watched Samantha. Her pointed nose wiggled as she ate. Like a rabbit. He thought of his friend Steve's rabbit, Snowy. It was an Angora, soft and gentle. Steve didn't live at the Home, of course. At the Home they didn't have rabbits.

"What are you thinking about?"

"Rabbits."

"I had a rabbit. I called him Flymo."

"Why?"

She snorted, spraying the table with coffee. "Because he kept the grass down!"

"Oh, very comical. Where is he now?"

She picked up her knife and fork and began to saw at the bacon. "Oh – he went away."

"Pet rabbits don't just go away. Not unless you let them out."

She shrugged, put a large square of bacon in her mouth and chewed stolidly.

"Well, did you let him out? I suppose you got bored with him," Matt said when she didn't answer. He could imagine that Sam, spoilt, probably given everything she ever asked for, would tire of things quite rapidly. "Don't you know that pet animals can't fend for themselves? A fox could have got him. Why didn't you just give him away if you were fed up with him?"

Sam flung down her fork. "Oh, stop asking stupid questions," she hissed, glaring at him with eyes suddenly cold as blue ice. "I get bored with stupid questions. And with stupid people!" Hands clenched and red gold curls quivering with rage, she looked as if at any moment she might leap across the table and physically attack him. Warily he asked her to pass the salt and made great play of eating his sausages and bacon.

There was no more conversation. After all, what could you say to a girl who blew up at the simplest question? It struck him that she was even more mixed up than some of his friends at the Home, and with far less reason. She *had* all anyone could want: a family, a big house and garden, her own horse, money. Really, she had no excuse for the way she acted, and if she thought she could snarl and yell at him just because she was a spoiled rich kid, then she was mistaken. As for her ridiculous tale of kidnapping, that was just talk.

As soon as he had finished his meal he would go. It had been a mistake to come here in the first place, and the sooner he was on his own again the better.

5

Roller Skates

As if she had read his thoughts, Sam sat bolt upright. "You're not going! I'm sorry I shouted, really I am. Look, I know something good we can do after lunch. Oh, please don't go!"

Matt hesitated. "Well -"

"Anyway, I promised to find you some dry clothes. Come on, let's go up to my room and you can try a pair of my jeans."

"I really should go," Matt protested as he found himself being half urged, half pushed, across the hall and up the staircase.

"And I've got a sweatshirt you can have. My favourite, it's from the Olympic Games -"

The jeans and shirt fitted well. He was grateful for them. It wasn't until he had peeled off his own clothes that he realised just how damp and uncomfortable they had been.

"You can have a bath if you like," said Sam.

"Thanks. Not just now." Lunch was one thing but somehow Matt felt that taking a bath in a strange house whose owners he had not yet met was going too far. He gazed at the soft white carpet and filmy white curtains, the fitted cupboards and crowded bookshelves. It was very different from the Home.

"What's *your* room like?" asked Sam.

"All right. I share with two other boys."

She wrinkled her nose. "I'd hate to share."

Yes, I bet you would, thought Matt. His eye was caught by a pair of framed photographs on a small table beside the window. "That your Mum and Dad?"

She came and stood beside him. "Yes," she said and together they looked down at the two faces. Mrs Cooper was a little like Samantha. The same narrow pointed face and the same springy halo of curls, but tidier. Mr Cooper had a moustache, the old fashioned sort that swept up at the ends. His hair was greying and he had a scar on one cheek, running from the corner of his mouth to his ear.

"That happened in Brazil," said Sam. Her finger traced the scar through the glass. "Some of the wild life got a bit too wild."

"What was he doing in Brazil?"

"Searching for new specimens – plants. Daddy's a botanist. He's quite famous."

She gazed at the photographs a moment longer. "Come on, let's go."

Back in the hall Sam produced two pairs of roller skates from a cupboard. "Put these on," she ordered, handing him a pair.

They were good skates, he saw, with large wheels crowded with ball bearings, and shiny chrome adjusters. As they sat on the hall stairs to fasten them he pinched himself. Was he really awake? Were there really people who skated in their own halls? Not in the world he moved in there weren't!

He stood up, expecting at any moment to see angry

adults rushing out of passages or sweeping down the staircase. But Sam confidently launched herself out into the centre of the floor with a loud whoop of pleasure and a rumbling roar of wheels that brought no response whatsoever from the empty silent rooms around them.

"Watch me!" she shouted. Catching hold of a pillar she swung round it, round and round, gaining speed until she was whirling in a dizzy blur. Then she let go and under Matt's astonished gaze flew off at a mad tangent towards the opposite wall where a lifesize Regency gentleman in lime green satin stared from his gilt frame in disapproval. Matt closed his eyes as the great portrait rocked violently and crashed to the floor. He was not surprised to see Irene appear at the door, but he *was* surprised when she turned back without a word and shut the door behind her. It was hard to believe that no-one cared.

Sam certainly showed no concern. She circled the hall a couple more times then advanced on Matt. "Well, come on then!" Grabbing his hand she began to tow him across the floor, and after one anxious backward glance he forgot everything except the pleasure of skating. Faster and faster they flew, forwards and backwards, side by side and in tandem, weaving between the stone pillars that supported the open gallery above. Matt felt wonderful. The rumble of the wheels filled his ears and the hollow echo of their shrieks, and even the damage they did, the new raw splinters in the oak floor, the vase that lay in pieces beside the stone fireplace, just added to his exhilaration. He shouldn't be skating here. But oh, it was fun!

Later came the guilt. As they flung themselves on to

the green brocade sofa that faced the front door Matt was dismayed at the havoc they had wreaked.

"Don't worry about it," said Sam with an airy wave of her hand. "Irene will sort it out."

Matt bent to unstrap the skates. "Look, I'd better be going. I want to find somewhere to stay before it gets dark."

Sam's mood changed instantly. "No! No, you can't go! Stay with me, please!"

"No, I really think - "

"We can have so much fun," she said desperately. "You must stay!"

"But why?"

"Because – I need a friend."

"OK, but you must have some proper friends. Why pick on me, we don't even know each other."

"I was at boarding school, all my friends are there. I don't have any round here."

Matt shook his head. He was beginning to feel trapped. She gazed at him pleadingly.

"Just stay till tomorrow. If you do, I'll lend you the money to go wherever you want. In fact, I'll give it to you. I've got nearly £100 saved up – enough to last you quite a while."

"Is that a promise?"

"I promise!"

"All right," he said reluctantly, "I suppose I could stay until the morning."

Sam's mood changed again. She sprang to her feet and clapped her hands.

"Brilliant! Now, what size shoes d'you take?"

"Six"

"Good, that's my size. You can wear my old boots. We're going riding."

"Riding? No thanks! I had enough riding this morning."

"But I'll lend you Bess. She's nice and gentle – not like Lucifer. You'll enjoy it, really you will."

Matt wasn't so sure. He had never ridden before and his introduction that morning on the back of Lucifer had been like learning to swim by being thrown off a ferry boat into the sea.

"You should be good," Sam flattered. "You've got the right build. And your hands look right too."

Matt extended his hands. They looked perfectly ordinary to him. Square, slightly tanned and slightly grubby, four of the finger nails bitten down.

"You're not really scared of horses, are you?" Sam challenged him.

"Of course not." Was he? No, only of falling off. But maybe riding a whole horse and not just the slippery back end of someone else's would be ok. Anyway, he was not going to be shamed by a girl – even one as weird as Sam. "All right, what are we waiting for?"

"Yeeks!" Sam leapt up. "Come on, then. Let's get those boots. Oh, and some clean socks. You're not wearing those wet smelly things inside my boots."

6

Matt meets Mr Higgins

Five minutes later they emerged into the corridor. But someone was about. As they turned on to the main landing Sam sighed. "It's Mr Higgins," she said in a disgusted whisper. "He's always snooping around."

Mr Higgins didn't look like a Mr Higgins. There was something un-English about the slanting cheekbones and the way he pursed his full mouth, red against the pale indoor olive of his skin. His dark eyes glittered as they rested on Matt and one well-manicured finger tapped lightly on the balustrade. But he wore the sort of English uniform Matt imagined a butler in a stately home might wear – black jacket, black and white striped trousers, a snowy white shirt and a striped tie.

"Who is this?" he asked Sam.

'He's my friend. He's staying with me."

"And your parents? They know?"

Sam snorted. "Come on, Matt . We're wasting time."

"Wait!" Mr Higgins' harsh command was a bullet in Matt's back and despite Sam's urging he stopped.

"Who are you, boy?"

"I – I - "

"His name's Matthew Jackson," said Sam swiftly.

"And he's a friend from school. It was all arranged ages ago, his parents dropped him off on their way to the airport. They've gone to Madeira for a week."

Matt had to admire her. He wished he could lie like that!

They did not come into the house." Half question, half statement.

"I was out riding. I met them outside the gates and they were already late, so they left him with me and dashed off."

"That is a pity," said Mr Higgins, "because I do not think your parents will wish to entertain your friend at this time. You know that they are extremely busy with their work."

"Well, we can't send him back," said Sam. "There's nobody to look after him. Even their housekeeper's gone off to stay with her sister. And there'd be an awful row if they came back and he wasn't here." Her eyes locked with Mr Higgins' and she spaced out her words. "They're very old friends of my parents. They know them very well. And Mr Jackson is a very important man. He has lots of contacts in the Government, the police - "

Mr Higgins was silent, but two more long white fingers joined the first to drum a tattoo on the balustrade. It was the only sound in the room and Matt found himself putting pictures to its rhythm: a train hurtling down a track faster and faster; a horse galloping downhill.

Sam dug him with a sharp elbow. "Let's go, look, the sun's shining and we're missing it."

Matt risked a glance at Mr Higgins but the man was

still staring at Sam. "A week, you say? Very well." Mr Higgins nodded, but there was no approval in his nod and Matt had an uncomfortable feeling that the matter was not ended.

"Use your knees," instructed Samantha. "And hold the reins the other way up."

"I feel like an idiot."

"You don't look it. You look great. Really. Now, straighten your back, that's it." She laughed. "I wish I had my camera here, I'd take a picture to show you. Really, you look an absolute natural."

"That's all very well, but looking natural isn't going to help me when we move. I still feel as if I'm going to fall off."

"You'll be all right." Sam moved her horse closer to his. "Now, do the same as me." She dug her heels into Lucifer's sides and with a click of her tongue and a light shake of the reins moved forward.

Matt imitated her actions. Bess, the dappled grey mare that Sam had produced for him, smiled placidly into space. "She doesn't want to go."

"You have to show her you mean it."

Matt tried again, and again, and at last they moved off across the stable courtyard towards the drive. He began to enjoy himself, letting his body sway lazily in the saddle. If he closed his eyes he could almost imagine he was a cowboy on a Texas ranch or the Australian Outback. He leaned forward and drew one hand down Bess's long grey neck, hot and slightly tacky against his palm. He inhaled her sweet horse smell and decided there was something in this riding business after all.

Really, it was quite easy once you had the knack.

The sky had cleared and the sun sparkled off grass still damp from the morning's rain. The smell of summer filled the air. Matt caught Sam's eye and they smiled at each other.

"Good, isn't it?" she said.

"Great." He clicked his teeth and to demonstrate his mastery dug his heels once or twice into Bess's sides. Bess ambled on.

Sam's smile broadened into a grin. "Race you to the gates!" she shouted.

"No! Hey! Help!"

Lucifer leapt forward. Bess, casting placidity to the wind, followed hot on his tail. Somehow Matt managed to cling on as the two horses galloped down the drive, gravel skidding beneath their hooves, but almost before he had time to feel real panic they had reached the tall wooden gates. Sam pressed the button.

"Come on," she said impatiently when nothing happened. She pressed again. "Would you believe it?" she said at last. "He's locked us in! He's fixed the gates so we can't get out!"

There followed another headlong gallop back to the yard, where Sam flung Lucifer's reins at Matt with an order to unsaddle and stable him and stormed off to the house.

What a pain, he muttered as he struggled with unfamiliar buckles and avoided Lucifer's questing teeth. Really, who did she think she was? Just as he was getting the hang of it, too. What did it matter if the gates wouldn't open? It wasn't the end of the world. They could have ridden round the garden, Heaven knows there was enough of it.

After he'd settled the horses, he followed her voice, shrill with anger, across a terrace bright with geraniums to an open French window. There he hesitated. The prospect of another encounter with Mr Higgins was not a pleasant one. He hid in the shadow of an overhanging tree and peered into the room.

The room was large, furnished with chairs and sofas and bookcases and small tables crowded with ornaments. More paintings hung against crimson walls, including one over the fireplace of Sam's father, younger and without his scar. Beneath the painting stood Mr Higgins, his olive face inscrutable but those telltale fingers of his beating out a slow tattoo on the marble mantel. His dark eyes followed Sam's furious pacing, back and forth, back and forth across the crowded room. Careless of anything that stood in her way, her waving arms swept a porcelain group of shepherdesses to the floor. Matt watched a tiny white head roll beneath one of the chairs.

"I have told you, Samantha," said Mr Higgins, "the gate mechanism is broken. Tomorrow it will be repaired."

Sam halted before him. Her red gold hair stood on end and her eyes glittered. "Oh yes! And when tomorrow comes it will be the next day and another excuse. I know what your game is – you think that now I've got someone on my side you'd better keep us locked up so we can't cause any trouble. But you won't get away with it, you – you old toad!"

Mr Higgins' fingers ceased their drumming. His eyes froze to black ice. "It must make Mr and Mrs Cooper most unhappy to see and hear such rudeness in their daughter. I am sure they have some suitable punishment in mind." His voice sharpened. "Yes, Mr Cooper? Mrs Cooper?"

Matt craned forward until he could see the other two people in the room. They sat together on a small sofa at right angles to the window, looking as unhappy as Mr Higgins could have wished. But there was no mistaking their identity. Mrs Cooper's red gold hair was as bright as Sam's own. Mr Cooper's scar twitched as his eyes moved with strained attention between his daughter and Mr Higgins.

Well! So much for Sam's kidnapping story!

Mr Cooper nodded. Mrs Cooper nodded too.

"Er – yes," she said. "I think some sort of punishment.- Let me see now -" Her voice trailed away into an uncomfortable silence.

"Perhaps confinement to her room," suggested Mr Higgins silkily, "might teach Samantha to think more carefully before she speaks. Don't you agree, Mr Cooper?"

"Yes, er, I think that would be best, Samantha, just for a while."

"And who's going to make me?" demanded Sam. "You? You'd have to put down your whisky glass first. Or dear Mummy? D'you think we could drag her attention away from that Hello magazine for five minutes?" She laughed. "You two couldn't make me do anything! Look at you, you're pathetic! You're just dummies! Stupid dummies! Sitting there, letting *him* do what he likes."

Matt's jaw dropped.

"That's enough, Samantha!" Mr Higgins' eyes blazed

at her. "Respect your parents. They love you. And they have no wish to upset you." He gave a half smile. "But I have no such qualms, my dear. Of course, if you refuse the opportunity to contemplate your misbehaviour, there are other options ...."

Sam's defiance crumbled. "But what about my friend? What's he going to do?"

That was the moment when Matt still had a choice. He could creep off, find a way out of this strange household – or he could stay and give Sam some support. Not that he approved of her behaviour. He could understand her dislike of Mr Higgins – she was right, he *was* a toad – but her parents seemed harmless.

And then his moment of choice was gone. He must have made some noise for they all turned towards him and he found himself being ushered into the room.

"So this is our daughter's little school friend," said Mrs Cooper, losing any sympathy he might have felt for her. *Little*! "Er – Martin, is it?"

"Matt," Sam corrected. "You know who he is. The Jacksons. Don't you remember? It was all arranged three months ago. Matt gets prickly heat whenever he's in a hot climate so they arranged to leave him with us while they went to Madeira."

Once again Matt marvelled at her inventiveness.

"Ah." Mr Cooper nodded. "The Jacksons."

"Wasn't it with Mr Jackson in Tibet last year that you found that new species of orchid?"

"Ah yes, of course."

Sam smiled and her eyes slid towards Matt. She changed the subject abruptly. "Anyway, you can't lock me up when we have a visitor. It's not polite."

Mr Higgins turned his dark gaze on Matt. "I am afraid Samantha must take her punishment, but *I* would be happy to entertain you until she is free again. Unless of course as her friend you would prefer to share her period of contemplation? That could also be arranged."

Matt hesitated. Being holed up with Sam in her present mood was not something he looked forward to, but the prospect of being 'entertained' by Mr Higgins sent a shiver through him. What he'd really like to do was to say goodbye and go on his way, but Sam's makebelieve had made that impossible.

"I'll keep Sam company," he said.

Did he imagine the sigh of relief that escaped Mrs Cooper, or the murmur of approval from her husband? Certainly the tension that had built up in the room began to lessen, escaping with an almost audible hiss, like air from a leaking balloon. Suddenly they were all smiling. All except Sam.

"A friend in need is a friend indeed," quoted Mr Higgins with solemn reverence. Matt looked away from the mocking gleam in his eyes.

"Oh by the way -" Mr Higgins drew Matt's attention back to him, and Matt saw that he was holding at arms length the damp and crumpled clothes that he had discarded upstairs. "I assume these are yours?"

"You've been in my room!" said Sam. "You've no right!"

"My dear. You left your door ajar. But these -" He examined the dirty mud-caked clothes with distaste. "I am surprised that Mr and Mrs Jackson would deliver their son in such a dreadful state."

"He fell off my horse," said Sam quickly. "Into a

puddle. He's not a very good rider," she added in explanation.

Mr Higgins raised a sceptical eyebrow. It was clear that he didn't believe Sam's story and Matt waited but he said no more.

7

Locked Up

"I could kick myself," said Sam, after Mr Higgins had left them alone. "If I hadn't lost my temper they'd have had no excuse to lock us up. Now they've got us where they want us – out of the way! They'll be planning all sorts of things down there."

Matt wished she would stop play-acting. Why did she have to be so dramatic? Typical girl. Typical of some of them, anyway. She was like Alison at the Home. Worse. At least Alison didn't insist that you all had a part in the play!

Across the room, above the white desk on which stood the photographs of Sam's parents, a shelf of books made a bright splash of colour. He wandered over and inspected them gloomily.

"Haven't you any games we could play? Or cards, even? I learned a new game last week -"

Sam stamped her foot. "Aren't you listening to anything I say? Here we are, *imprisoned,* and all you can talk about is silly games!"

"Oh, for heaven's sake, you're the one who's playing silly games! First you tell me your parents have been kidnapped, which obviously isn't true because I've seen them, and now you try to make me believe we're being held prisoner! All right, that Higgins man is pretty weird and I wouldn't like to have much to do with him, but I can't see anything wrong with your Mum and Dad. They seem quite normal to me. *You're* the one that's all mixed up, and what's more I think you quite deserve to be locked up for an hour or two. You were pretty rude, after all. If I'd spoken to my Mum like that I'd have been grounded for a week -"

"Oh, you – you -" Sam stormed over to her bed and flung herself across it. "You're stupid! There's no point in talking to you."

"All right, don't!" Matt picked a book at random off the shelf. It was 'Ballet Shoes' by Noel Streatfield. He gazed at it with disgust and put it back.

A long prickly silence stretched between the two of them. Sam remained on her bed, sharp chin propped between two tightly clenched fists. He decided to ignore her until she simmered down.

He returned to the window and stared out across the grounds. He was beginning to feel hungry. The morning's fry-up seemed an age ago and he had eaten very little at lunch. He wondered just how long they would be kept locked up. Would they be let out for tea? Or would their jailors slip a tin tray with bread and water through a crack in the door? He sighed. He was being as fanciful as Sam.

Beyond a clump of trees some distance from the house he could see the top of another building.

"What's that over there?" he asked Sam, forgetting that he was ignoring her. "That old ruin beyond the trees?"

"The old Abbey." Sam's voice was grumpy.

"Nobody uses it any more, it's in too bad a state. Sometimes historians come and poke about, and once the BBC filmed an episode of Dr Who there. Last year – it was quite exciting really. Mummy and Daddy were -" She stopped, and then he heard her open a drawer behind him. "I've had enough of this," she said. "Come on, let's get out of here."

He turned and saw that she had a key.

"What are you doing? We'll get into even more trouble!"

"No, we won't," she said. "Just keep quiet." She put her finger to her lips and turned the key in the lock. "We're going to hide in the attics."

"But they'll come looking for us."

"They won't find us until we're ready to be found. I know these attics better than anyone."

The only attic Matt had known was the one in the house where he had lived with his Dad and Mum until she died. It had always seemed large to him because it covered the area of the three bedrooms on the floor below, and he had been allowed to use it as a playroom for as long as he could remember. It was well lit and apart from a couple of suitcases and some camping equipment the rest of the space was his. He and Dad had set up a model railway that stretched over half the floor, and a couple of winters ago they had spent the long dark evenings making models of buildings and fields and roads to surround it. Dad had sold the engines and track when he lost his job.

Later as he chewed on a hunk of bread, snatched from the larder before leaving, he thought about his father. What would he think when he heard Matt had run away? With a sharp stab of misery he recalled the last time he had seen him, two weeks ago in the bare cream-painted visitors' room at the Home.

Dad, who'd given up smoking years ago, had lit up as soon as the Matron, Mrs Doherty, had left them. He smoked in quick nervous puffs as if to raise a smokescreen between himself and Matt as he told him his plans.

"I can't hack it here any longer," he said. "Since your Mom died – I see her everywhere. I just miss her so much."

"Me too," whispered Matt.

Dad stubbed out his cigarette and lit another one. "And losing my job – if I could just get something else, maybe things would be different, but nobody wants me."

What do you expect? Matt thought silently. "If you could just stop drinking....?" he said.

Dad looked away. "I've been thinking of going back to the States. I reckon it would be easier there, nothing to remind me. And the folks are not so – so stiff and disapproving. I could make a fresh start, give up the booze."

"And me?" His father didn't answer and Matt felt the beginnings of panic. "You are going to take me with you, aren't you?"

"Of course, Matt, of course. But – it would be easier if you stayed here for a while, just until I fix myself up with a job and find somewhere to live."

"NO!"

"It won't be for long. I'll keep in touch, honest."

"Yeah, right. The odd postcard or phone call."

"I'll be back before you know it, sonny. I promise."

Promises. In the last year Matt had learned how unreliable they could be. Well, if and when his Dad did come, Matt decided, he wouldn't find 'sonny' there any more. The Home had only been bearable while he had Dad's visits and the hope that someday they'd be able to make a home together again.

Nowadays Matt tried not to think about the time before Mum died. The three of them had been so happy. Dad had settled into a good job, buildings manager for a large company headquarters after years working worldwide as a project manager on construction sites. Mum worked part time in a creche for babies and toddlers, and Matt was in his first year at senior school, making new friends, struggling a bit during French and English lessons but doing well at maths and football. Weekends were brilliant. Picnics and trips to adventure parks, the seaside, football matches, – always the three of them together, having fun, laughing.

Then, just a year ago, it ended. On one of her days off Mum had gone shopping in the nearest big town. A gang of older boys racing along the pavement had knocked her into the path of a bus and she had died before an ambulance could reach the scene.

After that all Matt could remember was the silence. The silent house, Dad sitting huddled in front of the television screen, the volume turned to mute, Matt sitting in his bedroom not knowing what to do, feeling it was wrong to play computer games or phone his mates. His mates were silent anyway – they didn't know what to say to someone whose Mum had been killed so suddenly and shockingly.

Then Dad lost his job. The company directors had

been sympathetic, giving him time to recover but in the end they'd told him they would have to let him go. Everything got bad then. No money for anything but the essentials, Dad out at night wandering the streets, calling into the local pub, coming back long after closing time.

In the end Social Services stepped in, suggesting Matt might be better off in a Home, just temporarily, of course, just until his Dad found his feet again.

Well Dad hadn't found his feet. He had found a room in a cheap lodging house, an off-licence where he could get his nightly bottle of booze and a dream of making good again in the States. And where did Matt fit in? He didn't.

8

Into the Attics

The attics at Craven Manor were very different. Dark except for the odd chink of light from between the roof tiles, they were crammed with old furniture, pictures and ornaments, chests, toys, and dozens of other objects Matt could only guess at in the darkness. The dust-laden air smelled of musty clothes, damp and mothballs.

"There's no electricity up here," whispered Sam, "but I've got lots of torches hidden away. Stay there while I collect a couple."

As she shuffled away he heard other noises. Mice, he guessed. Or even rats. He wasn't really scared, but all the same he curled his toes. He didn't fancy being bitten in the dark.

Then Sam clicked on two torches and came back to him. "Come on," she said. "Let's have some fun!"

Each attic led to another, and another and another, some quite small, others enormous. Matt lost count of how many he had passed through. His torchlight flashed on a dressmaker's dummy swathed in cobwebbed shawls. In the next attic a battered rocking horse, minus its mane and tail, lay on its side. There were travelling trunks covered with faded labels, rolled up carpets, things that sent human-like shadows in the light of the torch.

Matt had no idea where they were in relation to the

rooms below.

"We're over Great Aunt Dorothy's bedroom," Sam whispered. "Better tiptoe!"

"Who's Great Aunt Dorothy?"

"She's another of *them*," said Sam. "Honestly, you don't want to meet her!"

They passed through another three attics .

"We're coming to my favourite place," said Sam.

As far as Matt could see, they had reached a blank wall with just a low chest of drawers against it, but Sam bent down and moved it easily out of the way. "It's empty. I threw all the stuff out."

Behind the chest was a low opening. "You'll have to crawl," whispered Sam. Once through, she quietly pulled the chest back into place and hooked a piece of heavy tapestry curtaining across the opening. "Now we can light the candles."

There were a dozen or more of them, shoved into candlesticks of every shape and size, and Matt shone his torch as Sam produced a box of matches and shuffled between them.

As the candlelight increased, he saw they were in another large space but this one glowed with colour and gleamed with the silver and copper of the candlesticks. Sam had strewn the bare boards with rugs and old bedspreads in a rainbow of colours, crimson, emerald, purple and gold. Silk and velvet curtains were pinned to the walls with drawing pins, and an inviting tumble of cushions filled the centre of the floor. Carved and painted masks decorated the walls,. A huge dried snake hung between two beams.

Sam flung herself on to the cushions. "This is my

secret nest," she said. "I've got my I-Pad and all my favourite books and games up here, and nobody except me knows about it!"

Matt's mouth fell open with astonishment. It was Aladdin's cave, the Arabian Nights. All they needed was a genie with a magic lamp. God, she was lucky!

"Well?" she asked. "What d'you think?"

She didn't deserve it, the way she behaved. He turned away. "You want to be careful, with all these candles. You could set the whole house on fire."

Sam's hard hand thumped him between his shoulders. "Matthew Bright!" she hissed. "You sound just like Mr Higgins! Why are you being so mean?" He could feel her eyes boring into him.

"You're jealous, aren't you?" she said.

"Of course I'm not jealous. Well, maybe a bit," he admitted. "But – it's you. You just don't deserve any of this. This house, horses, your parents, everything you want. You don't appreciate any of it. You're just bossy and badtempered and boastful and rude to everybody -"

"And you're just a miserable little scaredy-cat who doesn't know how to have fun and enjoy himself! 'Oh, we mustn't do this, we shouldn't say that!' Honestly, I'm surprised you had the guts to run away from that Home!"

He stared at her. Was that really how she saw him? How others saw him?

"I'm not like that," he said. "At least, I never used to be. There've just been so many bad things happening lately."

"What sort of things?" she asked after a silence.

He told her. About his Mum dying. About his Dad's

drinking and losing his job. About the Home and the boys who bullied him and called him Matilda.

"And now my Dad wants to go back to the States and leave me here."

"He's American?"

"Yes. But he's lived in England for a long time. He met my Mum here and I was born here."

"Wouldn't you like to go with him?"

"Yes, of course. Dad's from California and it's a great place. We lived there for a while when I was very small, but my Gran was alive then and Mum missed her so we came back to England. Now, with Mum dead and his job gone, there's no reason for him to stay here."

"There's you," said Sam.

"But I'm not important to him any more. I don't think he'll come back for me once he's gone. He'll forget all about me."

She reached out a hand. "No, he won't. I bet he really loves you. He won't forget."

Matt's eyes stung and he wished she would stop being sympathetic. It was easier when she was being her usual bad tempered self.

His stomach gave a loud gurgle and he sighed. The lunch he had barely tasted seemed not just hours but days past. "Hey, I don't suppose you've anything to eat in here?"

They sat together on the heap of cushions, Matt with the tin of biscuits Sam had found for him cradled on his knees. Dinner, she told him, wasn't usually served before seven (*Seven*! he groaned) so Mr Higgins was unlikely to come looking for them for at least two hours.

"Do you really think I'm rude and bossy and all those

other things you said?" she asked through a mouthful of biscuit.

He thought. Yes, he decided. But she had been nice to him about his Dad. Maybe he should say something nice in return.

"I guess you're all right really. Maybe I was just being jealous, like you said."

"No," she said. "I have been rude and bad tempered and I'm sorry. It's because I've got problems too."

He saw that her face had crumpled.

"What sort of problems?"

He waited a long time for her reply. Then, her voice so choked that he wasn't sure he was hearing her correctly, she said: "Those people downstairs. They're not my real mother and father."

"Of course they are. I've seen their photos."

"They're not! They look like them, but they're not them," she cried. "They're – they're imposters!"

He sighed. She was off again. He looked down at his feet, wishing he was somewhere else. Honestly, she was crazy, she really was. He kept his eyes on his feet. He was still wearing the borrowed riding boots. They were beginning to hurt. Perhaps Sam had a pair of trainers he could wear.

She was really crying now, making snuffly sounds. He wished she would shut up. All the same, he couldn't help feeling sorry for her. Crazy or not, she believed what she said, there was no doubt about that. Her misery filled the attic like a wet cloud. He didn't know what to say. He said nothing.

After a while the noises stopped and he risked a cautious glance. It was a relief to see Sam scrubbing the tears away with the palm of her hand. He waited until she had given her reddened nose a long blow.

"Look," he said awkwardly. "You really should stop all this business, you only get yourself all upset. Why don't you see a doctor, or something? I'm sure someone could help -"

"You don't believe me. No-one does. Even the police didn't believe me."

"The police!" Matt choked on his biscuit. "You mean you actually went to the police and told them what you've just told me?"

"That's exactly what I did."

"And what happened? I bet they laughed at you."

"They did not. They drove me back here in a patrol car and asked to see my parents." She scowled. "And – and maybe I'd have been able to get them on my side – there was a nice woman sergeant who looked as if she'd at least listen – if that toad hadn't made me look such an idiot. By the time they left they were convinced I was practically a nutcase and that my dear so-called parents had hired Mr Higgins especially to see that I didn't do myself or anyone else any harm. Mind you, if they'd had a chance to see *her* it might have been different."

"Her?"

"Great Aunt Dorothy. She's supposed to be my long-lost great aunt. All the way from Brazil where she's lived for 40 years, ever since she married dear 'R-r-Roberto!" Sam swiped viciously at a spider dozing in its freshly spun web. Startled, it rolled itself into a ball then thought better of it and scuttled for safety. "Great aunt my foot! If you think Mr Higgins is weird, wait till you see Great Aunt Dorothy. No-one could believe *she* was part of a normal English family!"

"What did they do after the police went away?" he asked. "Were they angry?"

Her mouth tightened. "Yes."

"Did they punish you? Lock you up?"

Sam's mouth tightened still further. When at last she spoke it was as if the words were stuck in her throat like marbles. "If you must know, that's when Flymo disappeared."

Matt was shocked. "You mean they – Mr Higgins -" He stole another glance at the small tight face that reminded him in its tawny-framed narrowness of a young fox. Any moment, he thought, she would burst into tears again.

But was any of this true? Or was it another of Sam's strange fancies? Something told him that the bit about the rabbit was true, but the rest – surely that was just Sam being weird.

"I'm sorry about your rabbit," he said at last.

Sam gave him a long look. She shook her head. "You still don't believe me."

"I don't know. I don't KNOW! It all seems so – it just doesn't make sense. D'you think they're aliens or something? Maybe they've mutated. Or maybe they were left behind by that Dr Who crew – Hey, watch it!" he yelled as she flew at him.

"So -" he said after a while, "if they're imposters, what d'you think they're up to? Why are they here?"

"*I* don't know, do I?" she said crossly.

They didn't speak again until what seemed hours later, when Sam peered at her watch. "It's half six," she said. "We'd better go back."

9

Held Prisoner

They crept back to Sam's bedroom and locked themselves in. Just before seven o'clock Mr Higgins came to let them out.

"I expect you are both hungry," he smiled. "Well, Samantha's parents have agreed that you shall join us for dinner – although you do not deserve it, Samantha."

"You think we want to eat with you?" she flared. "I'd rather take my food to the stables and eat with the horses!"

His smile disappeared. "Perhaps it will come to that if you continue to misbehave!"

Mr and Mrs Cooper (or their substitutes – Matt peered at them closely – no, they had to be the real Coopers, the likeness was perfect) were already seated at the table when they went down. 'Great Aunt Dorothy' wasn't there and Matt wondered when he would meet her.

They ate in the dining room. Glancing round at the dark panelled oak walls and the dark brocade curtains Matt thought it was hardly more cheerful than the conservatory. The chandelier high above their heads did little to light the gloom. A grandfather clock struck the half hour and everyone jumped.

Later, after they'd served themselves from a large tureen of mushroom soup, Matt glimpsed Irene through the half open dining room door. She was carrying a tray upstairs. Why didn't the Great Aunt eat downstairs with the others?

It was a strange household. Everyone was silent. Unsmiling.

"You're not very talkative, Mummy dear," said Sam. "Poor Matt must be bored with all this silence."

Mrs Cooper put down her fork. "Oh, I'm sorry, Matt. I was thinking about something else. Er – how are your parents? Mr and Mrs Jackson?"

"But you're old friends, Mummy. Surely you know their first names?" Sam said.

Mrs Cooper looked helplessly at Mr Higgins.

"Dennis and Fiona," Sam said.

"Dennis and Fiona," Mrs Cooper repeated. "Yes, of course. I look forward to meeting them again after their holiday."

"That proves they're fakes!" hissed Sam in Matt's ear. "There are no such people as Dennis and Fiona Jackson!"

"You will not whisper at dinner," said Mr Higgins sharply. "It is very ill-mannered."

Silence descended again upon the table. Feeling distinctly uncomfortable Matt took too much soup on his spoon and slurped loudly. He looked up to apologise, in time to see Mr Higgins making furious faces at Mrs Cooper.

Matt was uneasy. He didn't believe Sam's fantasies, oh no. But all the same, something was wrong. He didn't know what it was but definitely something was wrong.

Everyone was grim, tense. It was as if they were all waiting for an explosion.

Perhaps this Higgins man had a hold over the Coopers. Perhaps he was blackmailing them, threatening them. Perhaps that explained the changes Sam saw in them. She couldn't expect people, even her parents, to remain cheerful and normal if they were being threatened.

He began to feel indignant. He hadn't asked for this, he had enough problems of his own, and he wished heartily that he had never met Sam in the woods, that she hadn't persuaded him to come back to the Manor with her. Right now the last thing he needed was to get caught up in someone else's situation, one that might bring the police here.

After dinner they moved to the drawing room where Mr Cooper headed straight for the whisky decanter and poured himself a large measure. Mrs Cooper took a seat by the empty fireplace and began to flip through a magazine. Mr Higgins was restless, moving round the room, touching ornaments and books, twitching curtains. No-one spoke. Matt could sense Sam's tension as she sprawled beside him on the sofa pretending to read a book. He could almost feel sparks of electricity shooting from her.

Well, he'd had enough. Tomorrow morning he would find an excuse to leave . He had no idea where he would go, but he had to get away from this spooky house and this strange family before Sam involved him even more.

Suddenly she flung her book to the floor. "How can you go on like this? It's all make-believe! It's all -" She choked. "Well, you needn't think I'm going to be part of it! You make me sick, all of you. Look at you two – my parents! My 'father' drinking like a fish, getting tipsy every night, my 'mother' pretending she can read. My father would never get drunk, never! And my mother has a degree in anthropology – she doesn't spend her time looking at the pictures in trashy magazines and trying to read the headlines! And *you!*" She glared at Mr Higgins. "You absolute toad, some tutor you are! Why, you don't even know the difference between Dickens and Shakespeare!"

Mr Higgins moved towards her, his face thunderous.

Matt groaned. She was doing it again! Causing trouble. Why couldn't she just shut up? Hastily he ground the heel of his foot into her instep.

"OW! What did you do that for?"

He glared at her. "Because you're behaving like the worst sort of spoilt rich kid! How can you talk to your parents like that? You don't deserve to have any!"

Sam's mouth fell open. "But - "

He stood up. "This isn't turning out to be my idea of a holiday. I thought you were OK at school, but you're just behaving like a brat and I don't see any point in staying. In fact, I think I'll ring my Uncle Dan in the morning and get him to collect me." He turned to the Coopers. "I'm sorry. Thanks for offering to look after me but I think it'd be better if I moved on, if that's all right?"

The Coopers looked at each other uncertainly. "Well, we - " started Mr Cooper.

"Perhaps we can talk about it at breakfast," said Mr Higgins smoothly. "In the meantime I suggest we end the evening now. I will show you to your room, Matt."

Sam's face was a picture of betrayal. Matt tried to ignore it as he politely wished the Coopers good night, but he could feel her eyes boring into his back as he followed Mr Higgins up the stairs.

The stupid fool, he raged to himself. She was going to spoil everything. Mr Higgins was sharp as a razor, and it was obvious that he was the one in charge. If he thought Sam had told Matt her wild stories and that Matt believed her he could well make things awkward for him in the morning.

"I hope you will find this comfortable." Mr Higgins opened a door at the end of a corridor on the first floor. "You have your own bathroom so there is no need to lose yourself searching for one amongst all these rooms."

Aah, so he *did* suspect. Matt's heart sank.

"I really would like to leave in the morning," he said. "Sam and I haven't got a lot in common – I think I'd prefer to be with my Uncle Dan."

"And where does your Uncle Dan live?"

"In – in London."

"And where in London?"

Matt gave the first place he could think of. "Mayfair."

"Ah! A wealthy man, your Uncle Dan."

"N-not really. Actually, he's a – a chef." Matt wondered if he would ever be able to lie without stammering and blushing. "A chef," he repeated. "In a big hotel."

"And the name of the hotel?" Mr Higgins persisted.

"I – I can't remember. I only know his telephone

number."

"Hmmm. Well young man. Perhaps I will contact this Uncle Dan for you in the morning. I suggest you take the opportunity for a long sleep tonight, as you may have such a long journey tomorrow. All the way to Mayfair, London!"

Mr Higgins smiled mockingly and closed the door.

Matt glanced around the room. It was large but simply furnished, with a single bed, a desk and comfortable chair, a dressing table and an outsize mahogany wardrobe. The window was large but the casements were fitted with Chubb locks and there was no sign of a key in any of the drawers. He inspected the bathroom. It was well fitted but there was no window.

After a while he crept over to the bedroom door and tried the handle. Well, at least he wasn't locked in, that was a relief, but he had better not try to reach Sam's room, even if he could remember exactly where it was. He was sure Mr Higgins would be on the watch for that. But if he could stay awake long enough there might be a chance to get away once everyone was asleep.

Fully dressed he lay under the bedcovers and listened for what seemed hours to the faint noises of the house, creaks, footsteps, the murmur of voices. At last, when his watch showed two o'clock and the sliver of electric light from the landing had gone he felt confident that everyone was asleep, and slowly, stealthily, he left his bed and made his way across the room.

Just as he reached for the door handle he heard a strange humming sound and he snatched his hand away. He waited, listening to the sound dwindle away into distance, then opened the door. He was just in time to see the tail end of a wheelchair disappearing into a room at the end of the corridor.

Great Aunt Dorothy? he whispered to himself.

He waited another five minutes but there was no other sound in the house. Carrying his shoes he crept down the great staircase and across to the front door. It was locked. More Chubb locks. No escape there.

Turning, he crossed to the door leading to the kitchen. The kitchen was empty, but again the outside door was firmly locked. He backed away and looked around the big room. One of the cupboard doors was larger than the others, stretching from ceiling to floor. Opening it he saw a flight of stone steps leading down to the basement. Silently he crept down the stairs and began to explore.

The first door he opened led to a larder: shelf after shelf of tins and packets rising to the high ceiling. Enough for a siege, he thought. Perhaps that was what Mr Higgins and Irene were expecting.

The second room, smaller, was a vegetable store. There were two large sacks of potatoes in the corner, and racks held root vegetables. Strings of onions were suspended from hooks and along the length of one shelf stood boxes of apples. Matt's stomach reminded him with a gurgling rumble that it was several hours since he had eaten dinner. He stared at the apples; they were those crisp green ones with just a flush of pink. His fingers itched.

Crunch! The noise was unnervingly loud and for an anxious moment he held the large juicy bite of apple motionless between his teeth, but no-one stirred.

The third room was empty but the fourth fulfilled his

hopes. Ropes, tools, even a ladder. And, an added bonus, it had a door opening into the garden and the only locks were bolts on the inside. With a sigh of thankfulness he stepped into the room.

He had read about people's hearts sinking but he had never believed that it could actually happen. Until now, as he felt the sudden grip of hard bony fingers on his arm.

"Sleepwalking, Matthew?" asked Mr Higgins softly. "Let me escort you back before you wake up."

Matt said nothing.

10

Great Aunt Dorothy

No-one mentioned his attempted breakout next morning. It was as if nothing had happened. Mr Higgins seemed quite amiable for a change. Mr and Mrs Cooper made a little conversation about the weather, and Irene marched in and out, slapping plates of toast and jars of marmalade and honey on the table. Only Sam was different. She refused to look at him and her face was pale and set.

After breakfast he asked Mr Higgins if he could use the telephone. Mr Higgins smiled. "I am so sorry, Matt, the telephone line is down. Did you not hear the storm last night?"

"Storm?" There had been no storm, Matt was sure.

"Around five o'clock in the morning? It kept me awake for at least half an hour."

"Then – a mobile? Surely one of you has one?"

"Alas, there is no signal in these parts." Mr Higgins waved his hand vaguely. "So many tall trees. However, Irene has offered to drive into town later and inform British Telecom."

"Couldn't I go with her? I could phone from town."

Mr Higgins shook his head. "I am sorry. You are in our care, and it is best if we speak to this Uncle Dan personally and make sure the arrangements will be suitable, as your parents are out of the country."

So that was that. He really was a prisoner, for as long as Mr Higgins wanted to hold him. And it was all Sam's fault. She had tricked him into coming here, pretending she would help him

"Can we go out in the garden?" he asked.

"Of course," agreed Mr Higgins. "But first I believe that Samantha's Great Aunt would like to make your acquaintance. She sends her apologies that she has not welcomed you sooner, but as you may know, she is confined to her room."

Matt's heart jumped. Why should she want to see him? And why now?

"Go. You are keeping her waiting." Mr Higgins pushed him towards the staircase. "The last room on the left. She is expecting you."

Matt knocked and opened the door. The room was dimly lit, green blinds half drawn at the window. The furniture – a double bed, a writing table, bookshelves, a wardrobe – was all placed around the edges of the room, leaving the centre clear. There were no chairs. He noticed a sweet smell in the room and took a moment to identify it. Chocolate.

As his eyes became accustomed to the dimness he saw something bulky in the corner, motionless. Then the hum of wheels and Great Aunt Dorothy moved forward to greet him.

"Matt! How pleasant to meet you at last. Forgive the delay but as you see, I am not able to come downstairs easily."

"I – I – pleased to meet you too," he said faintly. He

tried not to stare at the grotesque figure in the wheelchair. Great Aunt Dorothy was immense. He thought she was probably the fattest person he had ever seen. Her flesh – so much flesh that it overflowed the sides of the chair – was swathed in black, and in spite of the warmth of the day a fur cape hid her shoulders. Her dark hair was coiled in an elaborate pyramid of curls, held by a large tortoiseshell comb. Against the startlingly white flesh of her face her eyes were sharp and black as basalt. On her lap was a large open box of chocolates. A plump hand hovered over it, chose and popped one into the scarlet circle of her mouth.

"My weakness," she said. "I cannot resist!"

He stood before her, awkward and apprehensive, as she ate another two chocolates.

"I am sorry there is no chair for you," she said. "As you see, I need space for my wheelchair."

"That's all right," he mumbled.

"You may sit on the bed," she said.

He stared at the rumpled satin sheets. A heavy musky scent rose from them. "It's ok. I'm happy to stand."

She took another chocolate.

"You know," she said when she had sucked it and wiped her lips, "Samantha is such an excitable young girl. I dote on her but she is a worry to us all. So much imagination! So much silliness! At this very moment she is punishing us. And you know why?"

"Er – no, I don't."

She leaned forward, brandishing the chocolate box at him. "Because her devoted mother and father have removed her from that boarding school. Because they have missed her and want to spend time with her. And because of that, she has disowned them! Disowned them! And I too – I who held her in my arms when she was no more than a week old!" She shook her head sadly. "There is no gratitude in the young!"

Matt hunted for something to say. "I think – I think she's just a little mixed up at the moment. I – I'm sure she loves you all really." He watched her select another chocolate. He understood now why Sam had said no-one could imagine her as part of an English family. Everything about her was so – so un-English. Even more so than Mr Higgins.

"Sam says you lived in South America?"

"I was born there. My father was the youngest son of Samantha's great grandfather. He was a missionary in the Brazilian forests. When he died I moved with my mother to Rio de Janeiro and met my dear Roberto, but every year I came to England to see my beloved relatives. Not for the past three years – my health has been too poor. Too many chocolates, perhaps!" She took another.

"Then, when my darling Edward, Samantha's father, arrived in Rio I decided there was nothing to keep me there any longer, Roberto had gone – pouf! - and so at Edward's invitation I came here."

It all sounded quite plausible.

Great Aunt Dorothy sighed sadly. "We worry for Samantha. I, her loving parents, even Mr Higgins – we worry she will do something silly. Harm herself – perhaps something even worse?"

Matt shook his head violently. "No. I'm sure she won't."

The Great Aunt sighed again. "I hope you are right.

But you will help us, yes? Help us to keep her from harm?" She waited.

He nodded, speechless.

"And you will let us know if she tries to spread nasty stories about us? Silly stories! Spiteful stories!" Her plump fingers jabbed at another chocolate.

He nodded again.

"Very good," she said, and waved the almost empty box below his nose. "You will have one, yes?"

"So what did you think of Great Aunt Dorothy?" asked Sam. She was hovering at the foot of the stairs.

Matt glanced round quickly. He couldn't see anyone but he had the feeling that they were being watched.

"She was telling me about her life in South America," he said. "I thought she was nice."

"WHAT?"

"Nice," he repeated loudly. "We got on quite well. She thinks a lot of you. Worries about you."

Sam looked at him as if he was mad.

"Come on," he said. "Let's go for a walk."

She shook her head mutinously. "No thanks."

"Oh come on," he coaxed. "I'm sorry I got angry with you."

In the end she agreed and they set off under the watchful gaze of Mr. Higgins. Once they were out of earshot Matt spoke.

"Actually I thought she was really creepy. She wanted me to keep an eye on you, seemed to think you might harm yourself."

"Hah!"

"Look, I'm sorry about last night," he said. "but I had

to stop you. I had to convince Mr Higgins that I didn't believe anything you might have told me."

She sniffed. "Well, that shouldn't have been hard. You *don't* believe me, do you?"

"No, I don't. I think there's something funny going on here, but I can't believe those aren't your real parents."

"I thought you were my friend!"

"How can I be your friend? We've only known each other a couple of days, and quite honestly I think you're a real pain. And I don't like the way you tricked me into coming here, telling me you'd help me."

"I didn't trick you. And I was going to help you, I've got the money in my room upstairs. I just thought you might be able to help me first. Anyway," she said sulkily. "what's the hurry to get away? It's not as if you've anywhere else to go."

"Maybe not, but I certainly don't want to stay here. I want to get on with my own life."

"Go on then. See if I care!"

"If you hadn't opened your big mouth last night -"

"I didn't! I just -"

"Oh, let's not argue," he snapped. "Look, I'm sorry but I have to go. Or try, at least. In a place this size there must be some way of escape."

He stuck his hands in his pockets and with an assumed nonchalance he was far from feeling he began to stroll across the lawns, stopping occasionally to peer at the sky or to pull and smell a flower. Once past the first shrubbery, however, he began to run. Sam's footsteps pounded behind him and he cursed, but the boundary wall lay ahead. What he needed was a medium size tree to climb and he would be up there on top. Never mind the long drop on the other side; he'd worry about that later.

When he reached the wall he was breathless, but he had no intention of resting. With Sam trailing after him he followed the course of the wall around the garden. He had travelled some three or four hundred metres inside the wall before he felt the first twinge of anxiety. Trees were there in plenty but none was nearer than ten metres to the wall. Only a few sawn stumps remained of those that had been closer, and he could only assume they had been deliberately cut down to prevent any possibility of escape by such a method.

Stubbornly he continued but each step only confirmed his suspicions. Finally, sick at heart, he realised they had come full circle and were back at the high wooden gates.

"I could have told you you couldn't get out," said Sam smugly.

He glared at her. Really, she was the most infuriating girl he had ever met.

"If you knew, why didn't you say?"

Her sharp chin jutted. "Why should I? Half the time you don't believe what I say, and the rest of the time you shout at me!"

"No I don't. It's just – oh, it's impossible to talk to you! This isn't a game, you know!"

He stomped over to the gates, picked up a handful of gravel and threw it in a gesture of useless fury at the solid iron-bound wood.

He flung himself down on the grass and tried to think. There was no way out except through the gates or over the wall. The wall was finished in smooth grey cement, not a finger or toe hold in sight. Barbed wire and jagged chunks of glass were embedded in the top. But the gates although tall and built of smooth solid vertical planks, could easily be scaled with a ladder. And he knew where to get one.

If someone could keep the others busy, he could sneak into the basement, steal the ladder and hide it somewhere in the grounds until after dark.

There was someone. Sam.

11

Matt Overhears a Plot

"I'm not going to help unless you take me with you," Sam said.

"That would be stupid. Your family is well known. We'd have the whole police force searching for us. And two of us would be easier to spot. If I'm alone I'm less likely to be noticed."

"But you can't go without me, I won't let you!"

"You can't really stop me."

"Yes I can! I'll tell on you!"

"Now how stupid would that be? Then we'd both be kept prisoner."

She glared at him, tears brightening her eyes. "You don't care about me. All you care about is yourself! You're like a – you're like a rat deserting the drowning ship!"

"Sinking," he murmured.

"What?"

"Sinking, not drowning. It's the rats that drown. Anyway, you'd slow me down. I can run faster than you."

"No you can't! Watch me!" And she took off at high speed along the drive. He had to admit she could run, but he still had no intention of taking her with him. Sam was impulsive and hot-tempered and acted without thinking.

He couldn't rely on her to be quiet and sensible.

He waited, but she didn't reappear. He sighed. *Now* what was she up to? He waited another five minutes, then turned to go back to the house.

There was no sign of her on the terrace or in the conservatory. Perhaps she was sulking in her bedroom. Not wanting to meet any of the others, he crept as quietly as he could up the stairs.

Sam wasn't in her room, but he heard voices and they were coming from Great Aunt Dorothy's room. He tiptoed towards the door and listened.

He heard Mr Higgins first.

"The Coopers have set up the final tests," he was saying. "All that is needed is for them to document the formula, but they are being a little obstructive. They will need persuading."

"How?" That was Irene's voice.

"They want to see Samantha again. They say they will not let us have the formula until they see that she is still alive." Mr Higgins laughed. "For some reason they do not trust us!"

"Then take the girl to them," said Great Aunt Dorothy impatiently. "Let them see each other. What does it matter? Once we have what we want, they will all be dead – pouf!"

Matt froze.

"What about the boy?" Mr Cooper this time.

"We will kill him too. He is nothing, a runaway from a Home. No-one will miss him."

"I thought he was a school friend of Samantha's," said Mrs Cooper.

Mr Higgins laughed. "Another of Samantha's lies. It

was obvious to me when I found his clothes that no friends of the Coopers would deliver their son here in such a state, dirty, dressed like a street urchin and covered in mud. No, I was sure that the boy was not what he seemed, and when I listened to the local news on the radio all became clear."

"And what about us?" asked Mrs Cooper. "When can we leave?"

"You leave with us. We all fly back to Rio. After that – you may do what you wish." That was Mr Higgins again. "Don't worry. You will both be well rewarded."

"How do we know you won't kill us too?" asked Mr Cooper.

"Why should we?" said Mr Higgins. "You will be wealthy people. You can continue to live the delightful life of the Coopers, or you can choose to disappear. If you were foolish enough to say anything about us you would lose everything – and of course you would become prisoners yourselves. No, we have no reason to kill you."

"We are interested only in the drug," said Great Aunt Dorothy. "When I have the drug I will be – reborn. It is all I care about! The money – pouf!"

"You will have your drug, Mama," said Mr Higgins. "But we will have the money too."

Mama! Matt's jaw dropped. So Great Aunt Dorothy was Mr Higgins' mother – but of course Mr Higgins was not Mr Higgins. And the Coopers were not the real Coopers. And what about Irene? Who was she? Perhaps she was Mr Higgins' wife.

He heard movement from within the room He fled, reaching the front door just in time. He ran for the shelter of the shrubbery.

He crouched, making himself as small as possible. He felt physically sick. Sam had been right all along. If only he had listened. Now they were all in danger. Sam, Sam's real parents, Matt himself. Soon – but when? - they would all be dead.

Unless he could stop them. But how? The plotters numbered five, and there was only one of him. And he was only eleven. What could a boy of eleven do against a determined ruthless gang?

"What are you doing in there?" It was Sam, her sharp face pushed between the bushes, red gold hair on end.

"Hell!" She was going to ruin everything. "Go away!" he hissed.

"No I won't go away! I live here! What's going on?" she demanded loudly.

He pulled her into the thickness of the shrubs. "Be quiet and listen! I heard them talking in Great Aunt Dorothy's room and you were right. They're *not* your real parents."

"You – you believe me, then?" Sam's face split into a broad grin.

"Yes, but we can't talk here. If they hear us, I don't know what they might do."

"Did – did they say where my real parents are?"

"No, but -" Should he tell her what was planned? No, she might become hysterical and that would be the end of any chance of escape. "I think you need to tell me all you know. It might help us to find them."

"We'll go up to my attic then," said Sam.

They sat amongst the candles. Sam had produced another tin of biscuits. Matt took one and tried to listen patiently although everything urged him to rush downstairs and do something – anything – to stop the gang's plan.

"It must have started when they were in South America," she told him, ."but I'm guessing because there's no way I can find out. All I know is that until Mummy and Daddy went to Rio de Janeiro three months ago everything was marvellous, we had lovely times together and – Oh, I wish I'd been able to go with them! If only it had been a month later when my school had half term – if I'd been with them everything might have been all right."

"What were they doing in Rio de Janeiro?"

"Well, I told you Daddy was a botanist, didn't I? He's quite famous in fact, because he's discovered lots of new species and he's an expert on the use of plants and extractions – you know, in medicine and cosmetics and things. Anyway, he gets invited to conferences all over the world. Sometimes Mummy goes too if it's a new place, and sometimes they take me as well if it doesn't interfere with school. When they can't take me I stay here with Mrs Miles our housekeeper and Mr Herrick, Dad's secretary, to look after me.

"Well, the conference was due to last three days and after that Daddy planned to take a couple of weeks off. They planned to go off into the rain forests, looking for new specimens. Altogether they were to be away four and a half weeks and on the 7th July they were due back in England."

She stopped and took a deep breath. Matt urged her on.

"Well, about four days before they were due back Mr Herrick got a letter from Daddy. It was Daddy's handwriting, I'm sure of that because I saw the envelope, but I don't know what was inside. Whatever it was, it upset Mr Herrick and it wasn't long before everyone else was upset too. Mrs Miles, and Arthur who looked after the grounds and did odd jobs, and Mrs Fitt from the village.

"And that's when everything began to go wrong. Mr Herrick went off into town with a face like a thundercloud and Mrs Miles kept blowing her nose and saying it wasn't right, and Mrs Fitt broke three cups washing the dishes and then flounced back to the village still in her pinny. And Arthur, well, he pulled up the special little acer Daddy had brought back from Japan."

Sam had been home when the letter arrived – the school had given all the pupils a long weekend – but there had been no letter or message for her from either of her parents, which in itself was unusual. When Mr Herrick returned from town, however, she learned that all the household had lost their jobs, although none could or would give her a reason. He had a walletful of money from the bank - "An awful lot of money," she said – to pay them off. And then Sam was to be sent back by train to her school, there to be collected a day or two after her parents' return.

She became more and more convinced that something dreadful had happened, if not to her father, then to her mother – perhaps she had had an accident or contracted some awful tropical disease. Sam pleaded with Mr Herrick to explain, but he insisted that as far as he knew the Coopers were both in good health. He could think of no reason why they should sack such loyal employees.

"Well, Mr Herrick put me on the train for school," she continued, "and I stayed there for five days. It was miserable. Nearly everyone had gone home and I waited and waited, still not knowing what had happened. It seemed as if I would wait there forever , and then at last Mrs Topham, the Head, told me someone had arrived to take me home. It was Irene.

"She was all smiling and friendly then, and neatly dressed in a dark blue suit that I never saw her wear again. She told me she was our new housekeeper but she said she had no idea why Mrs Miles had left. She said she'd only just been hired and hadn't met any of the old staff.

"She bought me chocolates and a magazine for the train, and really she acted so nicely that I thought everything was going to be all right.

"And then when we got back to Craven Manor I met *them.*"

Matt waited but she was silent. Her fingers picked absently at the velvet pile of a cushion.

"Have you ever had one of those horrid dreams? When you know you're dreaming and you keep pinching yourself to wake up? But you can't and it goes on and on, a nightmare,. Well, it was like that.

"There were Mummy and Daddy in their usual chairs in the drawing room, smiling at me, saying hello and giving me presents. Daddy pouring whisky and ginger for himself and a Campari and soda for Mummy and a glass of lemonade for me, like we always had before dinner. Mummy was wearing a dark green skirt and a spotted blouse that I'd seen a dozen times before, and Daddy was very tanned. He always tans easily when he goes to a hot country, and his scar stands out pale pink. They looked exactly the same and yet – I wanted to run away from them. They were Mummy and Daddy – and yet, they were *not* Mummy and Daddy!" She put her hands over her face. "It was horrible!"

"Did you say anything?"

"No. It was so weird, I was frightened. And at that time I still wasn't sure. I mean – people lose their parents, they die or get killed or get divorced. But who ever heard of them being replaced by look-alikes?

"It was so crazy I couldn't believe it. And they kept saying things that no-one else could have known – you know, about my childhood or school. After a while I began to wonder if I was the one who had changed. Gone bonkers overnight!"

"How did they explain Mr Higgins and Irene?"

"They said their solicitor Mr Bernard had contacted them in South America. He'd found out that Mr Herrick and Mrs Miles had been dipping into the housekeeping money – Daddy trusted Mr Herrick completely and had opened a special bank account for him to pay all the expenses while they were away – and that probably Arthur and Mrs Fitt had been getting extra payments as well.

"Anyway, because my father had known them so long he decided not to prosecute. Instead they were all to get paid off with three months' wages and Mr Higgins and Irene were hired instead. Mr Higgins was to be my tutor, and from now on I would be taught at home.

"It's been horrible and I've been so scared." Her eyes filled with tears. "But now you're here and you believe me. It makes me feel a bit better."

"Yes, well – Look, I'm sorry," Matt said awkwardly "I wish I'd believed you sooner But if we can get away now we'll go straight to the police and tell them what's been happening."

"They wouldn't believe me last time."

"There'll be two of us this time."

"Even if they believe me, it may be too late to save my parents." She sighed. "I can't help thinking – thinking they might already be dead."

"No, they're definitely alive." (At the moment, he added to himself.) "They're being held prisoner somewhere."

"But where?"

He shrugged helplessly.

"They could be anywhere," she said at last. "Anywhere in the world."

12

The Flood

"We have to get out," said Matt. "If I can get the ladder from the basement, we could use it to scale the wall. If I can just get it there without any of them seeing me we could sneak away after lunch."

They were sitting in the conservatory, at the far end away from any listening ears. "We need a diversion", he said. "Something that will bring them all together somewhere while I nick the ladder."

"I can do a fainting fit," said Sam. "I'm good at that. It used to come in useful at school when we had hockey."

"I can't see them all rushing to your aid just for a faint."

"No, you're right, they all hate me. They'd probably be glad I was quiet for a while."

"You're right there!"

She glared at him.

The heat of the conservatory was making him feel sick. He felt trapped and irritable and without a single idea.

"We could light a big fire in the kitchen," said Sam.

"That's pretty dangerous. The whole house could burn down."

"A small one, then."

"If it's small, Irene could probably put it out on her own."

"Well, *you* think of something!"

"I can't," he admitted.

Out on the terrace Irene was watering tubs of geraniums with a hose. They watched as the sparkling water hit the geranium leaves and sprayed over the flagstones.

"I've got it! What about a flood? Upstairs in one of the bathrooms." Sam grinned mischievously. "Actually, there's one right over the dining room. If the water soaked through the ceiling right on lunchtime, that should put them all in a tizzy and you should be able to sneak away."

"Brilliant – but we'd better start it now, it's already eleven."

Even with the taps on at full pressure the huge Victorian bath took ages to fill. Impatient as always, Sam brought a large jug from the landing and began bailing water out of the washbasin and pouring it on to the floor.

They had taken the precaution of removing their shoes and socks and rolling up their sleeves, but Sam got excited and began to splash water at Matt.

"Stop it! We don't want any evidence on us," said Matt, "And for heaven's sake, be quiet! We don't want them to hear us!"

By eleven thirty the bath was overflowing . Sam turned the tap to a quiet trickle, bailed out the last of the water in the hand basin and pulled out the plug. The water was already spreading across the floor and finding its own level. They gazed at it with satisfaction.

"They're all going to get a lovely surprise later," said Sam.

They closed the door and retreated to Sam's bedroom to put on their shoes and socks.

"What about the Great Aunt?" asked Matt. "She'll still be in her room. I'll have to make sure I'm not in view of her window when I get the ladder."

"Her room looks over the front of the house," said Sam, "and the basement doors are at the back. You'll be all right."

At lunch Irene brought in bowls of salad, a basket of bread and a platter of mixed cold meats. Mr Cooper poured wine, large glasses, for himself and Mrs Cooper and Mr Higgins.

"Orange juice, Matt?" asked Sam. She gave him a wicked smile. "Or would you rather have water?"

Lunch was as silent as dinner the previous night. Mr Higgins ate little. He appeared deep in thought as he cut up and moved a slice of smoked chicken around his plate. The Coopers said nothing either. Mr Cooper looked tired and bored, while Mrs Cooper's glance flitted anxiously from face to face.

Matt resisted the temptation to stare up at the ceiling. Surely the bathroom flood should have soaked through by now? He checked his watch. They had been sitting at table for twenty minutes.

And then in the silence he heard the first loud plop. With perfect aim a drop of water had penetrated the ceiling and fallen into Mr Higgins' glass of red wine. Sam had to stifle a giggle as he stared at it in disbelief. It was soon followed by more plops as water seeped through in various places and trickled down into the salad, the bread, the drinks and the bowl of fruit in the centre of the table.

"What -" Mr Higgins sprang to his feet. He glared at Sam and Matt. "Has someone left a tap on?"

They stared back at him innocently.

But the result of Sam and Matt's efforts was even more spectacular than they had hoped. Suddenly with a tremendous crash the chandelier and a large part of the ceiling collapsed on to the table, showering crystals all over the room and spraying everyone with sodden pieces of plasterboard.

"What in hell?" Mr Higgins brushed at his dark jacket, Mrs Cooper screamed for Irene, then all three dived for the door.

"Go!" whispered Sam. "Out the French window." And Matt raced into the garden. He prayed that the door leading out from the basement was unlocked and it was.

The basement was empty and he grabbed the ladder from the toolroom. The ladder was of the fold-up type, easier to conceal but heavy to carry. It knocked painfully against his shins as he struggled up the basement steps to the yard above. He managed to reach a large clump of evergreens a short distance from the back of the house and thrust the ladder into its midst.

He was panting when he got back to the dining room and had to pause for a moment or two to control his breathing. He looked at his watch. It had taken him ten minutes. Had he been missed?

Inside the room there was a strong smell of wet carpet, and his feet crunched on fallen crystals. Towels and newspapers were strewn around the room to soak up the water and flakes of white plaster speckled the furniture. Sam and Mr Higgins were just returning.

"I'm *sorry!*" Sam was saying. "I just fancied a bath and then I got distracted. It could happen to anybody."

"No, Samantha," he said through gritted teeth. "Only to you! And look at the damage you have caused!"

"I'm sorry," she said meekly. "But we can get someone in to repair the ceiling, can't we?"

"The ceiling can wait," He unbuttoned his jacket and took it off, showing a grey and white striped shirt and red braces. "Tskk! My jacket is ruined!"

Behind his back Sam looked at Matt, one eyebrow raised. He gave her a thumbs-up sign.

In the commotion no-one noticed the insistent buzzing until there was one of those sudden silences when everyone stopped speaking at the same time.

"It's the gate!" yelled Sam and she ran from the room, hotly pursued by Mr Higgins, the Coopers and Matt.

Sam got to the hall first and grabbed the phone that connected the Manor gates to the house.

"Who is it?" she shrieked.

Mr Higgins tried to snatch the phone but she danced away from him.

"Mrs Bailey! How are you? It's Sam here … Yes, of course you can come in – I'm just pressing the button now."

Mr Higgins glared at her. "Who is this Mrs Bailey? And what does she want?"

"Oh, of course you wouldn't know, would you?" smiled Sam. She turned to the Coopers. "But *you* know, don't you?"

They stared at each other helplessly.

"Mrs Bailey?" Sam repeated. "From the Women's Institute? She organises the village fete every year. It's always held here. It's one of the biggest local events of the year – dog show, a jazz band, competitions, a disco in the evening. Great fun!"

"And when is this village fete?" asked Mr Higgins.

"Oh, you don't have to worry," said Sam. "It's not for another two or three weeks – the third Saturday in August. I expect Mrs Bailey just wants Mummy and Daddy to OK the plans. They don't actually have to *do* anything – except declare it open, of course. A gang from the village come and do all the preparation. You know, putting up stands, lights and so on. There'll be lots of them here," she said with satisfaction. "I expect they'll want to start any day now! "

Matt saw the glances of dismay between the Coopers.

"Well, she cannot come in," said Mr Higgins. "The gate mechanism is still out of order."

But at that moment the doorbell rang and Sam opened the door to a small panting figure, a bulging bag under her arm, a straw hat rammed on the back of her head.

"My goodness," she said. "I'm all out of puff! I'd swear your drive gets longer every year!"

Mrs Cooper took a breath and moved forward. "Mrs Bailey! How nice to see you again!"

"Ooh, how formal! Molly, *please*! You always call me Molly!" laughed Mrs Bailey.

"Molly, of course. But how did you get in?" asked Mrs Cooper.

Mrs Bailey waved a hair clip triumphantly. "Never

fails," she said. "But you want to get my Andy to see to that gate. Always going wrong, it is."

"I'm afraid you've caught us at a difficult moment. Our dining room ceiling has just fallen down."

"An accident with the plumbing," added Mr Cooper.

"Oh my goodness! Let's have a look." Mrs Bailey pushed her way across the hall. "Oh my word!" she gasped as she stood in the doorway of the dining room, "You'll be wanting my Andy to see to that too. I'll get him to come along in the morning."

"No, no," said Mr Higgins quickly. "We would not dream of troubling him. We will call someone in from town."

Mrs Bailey looked him up and down. "And who might you be?" she asked sharply. "Not from these parts, are you? Else you'd know we don't give our business elsewhere if we can help it. No, Andy'll be here tomorrow and he'll do a good job, you mark my words!"

"No!" Mr Cooper stood up "I'm sorry, Mrs Bailey – Molly – but I'm afraid it will have to wait. We have – something urgent to deal with over the next few days."

"Oh well!" Mrs Bailey pulled her coat closer and rammed her hat further on to her head. "In that case, if you're going to be so *busy*, we'd better deal with the paperwork for the fete today, Mrs C." And turning tail she marched off to the drawing room, settled herself on one of the sofas and tipped the contents of her bag on to the coffee table alongside.

The Coopers followed helplessly.

"I'd hoped she'd realise they're not my real parents," Sam whispered gloomily to Matt. "She's known them since I was eight, but she seems to have been taken in just like everyone else who's called here."

"I suppose when you're expecting to see someone and they look the same, there's no reason to be suspicious," he whispered back.

They hovered in the doorway while Mrs Bailey went through the details of the fete with the baffled Coopers.

"I'm going to write her a note," whispered Sam. "I'll sneak it to her when she leaves." She slid back into the hall and tiptoed across to the library. When she returned she gave Matt a glimpse of a tightly folded piece of paper.

At last Mrs Bailey gathered together her various notes and lists, stuffed them into her bag and rose to her feet.

Sam rushed forward and flung her arms round the astonished woman. "Lovely to see you again, Mrs B.," she said. "Give my love to Mr B. and Andy."

"Well, my word, it's nice to see you too, Sam. Will you be here for the fete?"

"You bet," said Sam.

At the front door Mrs Bailey paused. "Now, where did I put my specs?"

Matt and Sam held their breath as she rummaged through her large bag.

"Always mislaying them," she muttered, and then her hands were searching her coat pockets.

"They are on your nose," said Mr Higgins with cold politeness.

"So they are! Now, what's this?" She had pulled out Sam's note from her pocket and was unfolding it. "Dear me," she said.

"May I see?" asked Mr Higgins. He took the note

from her and scanned it.

Sam gripped Matt's hand.

"I must apologise for Samantha," said Mr Higgins after a long moment. "She is not herself at the moment. In fact she has been brought home early from school to recuperate – I am her temporary tutor. As you can see, she is suffering from some rather strange delusions."

Mrs Bailey gave Sam an uncertain glance. "Well, I'm sorry to hear that, dear."

"She is receiving the best of attention," said Mr Higgins smoothly. "A specialist from London. Rest and a course of tablets. That is all she needs. And now, Mrs Bailey, perhaps Mr Cooper will see you to the gate."

After Mrs Bailey had gone he turned to Sam, his face tight with anger. "What are we to do with you? Such a troublemaker. You cannot believe anyone will take your fancies seriously?" He shook his head. "Even your friend Matthew is tired of your behaviour and wishes to leave. Is that not so, young man?"

Matt nodded.

"Well, tomorrow we will most certainly contact your uncle and arrange for you to be collected."

Matt nodded again. He wondered gloomily why Mr Higgins was still keeping up the pretence. It was quite obvious that he had no intention of letting either him or Sam go.

"In the meantime," Mr Higgins continued, "how can we entertain you whilst Samantha spends a quiet hour in her room?"

"I don't need entertaining. I'll stay with Sam."

"I think not," said Mr Higgins. "I think it is best if you spend some time apart. There is a library full of excellent books across the hall. Perhaps you would like to use the time by improving your knowledge?"

Not an exciting prospect but Matt thought it might give him another opportunity to escape. "All right," he said.

After Mr Higgins had left he checked the door. He wasn't surprised to find it was locked. The library was a large room with windows on two sides, surrounded by bookshelves. Matt estimated there must be several thousand books at least, and wondered if the Coopers – the real Coopers – had read them all.

Without much hope he crossed to the windows. He thought it unlikely that they would have left one of them unlocked but patiently he began to check the casements. His patience was rewarded. One of the upper casements, large enough for him to climb through, had been left on the latch. Across the room he saw a combination stool and steps, tall enough to enable him to reach it.

In less than a minute he was outside, throwing himself behind one of the seats on the terrace while he checked if he had been seen. He would stay out of sight until he was absolutely sure all the others were in the house.

He was about to leave his hiding place when Mr Higgins and Irene appeared. Mr Higgins was carrying a bulky bag over his shoulder. The pair looked around them carefully before they set off across the lawn.

Where were they going? What were they up to? Deciding to follow them, Matt dodged from bush to bush, careful to keep out of sight of the house windows. They were making for the ruined Abbey.

Just outside the walls of the Abbey there was an area

of broken stone paving, overgrown with weeds and brushwood and self-seeded shrubs. The two stopped there and Matt flung himself down amongst a crop of brambles and nettles, just before Mr Higgins turned to survey the landscape.

"Ouch!" Matt whimpered silently but he forced himself to stay motionless until Mr Higgins was satisfied.

Irene bent and pulled away the brushwood and Mr Higgins produced a key. Matt raised his head cautiously. He watched as Mr Higgins undid a padlock and heaved up a sturdy trapdoor. He held his breath as the two descended into whatever lay below.

So this was where they were holding the real Coopers! It made sense. Out of sight. Out of hearing, he guessed, yet close enough for the gang to control. But what was below the trapdoor? There must be a tunnel, he decided, leading into the old Abbey ruins. Would there be a crypt? Sam had told him the Abbey was unsafe and no longer used, but perhaps the crypt was still intact. A perfect hiding place. And once the gang had what they wanted, an even more perfect burial place for the bodies. The Coopers. Sam. Himself. They would all be killed and hidden below ground.

Matt guessed that Mr Higgins had planned a false trail already. The fake Coopers would make a great show of returning to Argentina. As for Samantha – well, it would be easy to spread word that she had gone to stay with friends.

No-one would suspect the truth. He felt sick.

There was nothing he could do. Or was there? He raised his head again. There was no sign of Mr Higgins and Irene, and he could see that they had closed the trapdoor behind them. If he could lock the pair in the crypt, that would give him time to get the ladder and he and Sam could make their escape. Once they were free they would somehow contact the police and lead them back to the Manor. Surely the police would believe the two of them.

He crept closer to the trapdoor and reached for the padlock. It was not there. Mr Higgins, it seemed, thought of everything and he had taken it below with him.

Matt hovered, bitter with disappointment, unsure what to do next. There might still be time to get away on his own and he was tempted to have a go. On the other hand, how could he leave without letting Sam know her parents were here? He would have to go back to the house, he decided.

13

The Secret of the Abbey

When he reached Sam's room he knocked gently on the door.

"Who is it?" she asked loudly.

"Sssh! It's me. Let me in."

"Wait. I'll get my key."

"Promise you won't get all hysterical," he said, once he had slipped inside.

"I never get hysterical."

"Yes, you do!"

"I don't!"

"Oh, just shut up, Sam. I've got something important to tell you. They're here!"

"Who's here?"

"Your parents! They're locked in some place under the Abbey."

Sam's eyes widened. "The old crypt? But the entrance was blocked up years ago. It wasn't safe."

"Well, I saw Mr Higgins and Irene pulling open a trapdoor just outside the walls. They took something down there. Food, I suppose."

"Another way in – I'd no idea. Oh, poor Mummy and Daddy, all this time down there in the dark and I didn't know!" Sam gripped Matt's arm. "We have to rescue them! Come on!"

"No! We daren't risk it in daylight. We'll wait until tonight when they're all asleep."

"No, we have to go now! Please!" Sam was crying. "I have to see them!"

"Sam, Sam! Be quiet, someone will hear you!"

She squeezed her eyes shut, took a deep breath and held it until all that was left was a small hiccup. "Sorry."

"We must behave absolutely normally all day," Matt warned her. "They mustn't suspect that we know, otherwise we'll all ...."

"All what?" she asked.

"The thing is – the thing is -" He paused. If he told her what was planned, she was sure to have hysterics. But he couldn't *not* tell her, it wouldn't be fair.

"The thing is, they're planning to kill us. All of us."

Sam's face turned white. Her mouth opened and closed. "But -"

"Sssh!"

"When did you find out?" she whispered.

"When I listened at Great Aunt Dorothy's door."

"Why didn't you tell me sooner?"

"I'm sorry. I wasn't sure how you'd react. I thought it best you didn't know. I'm sorry."

She was silent for long minutes. "Well, you'd better tell me everything now," she said at last.

Matt proceeded to tell her what had been planned. Neither of them heard the humming outside the room. Neither of them noticed the slow turning of the handle and the inch by inch movement of the door until suddenly it slammed open and Great Aunt Dorothy and her wheelchair filled the doorway.

In the brighter light of Sam's room she was an even more disturbing sight. Thick white powder clogged the heavy folds of her face and neck. Against the whiteness her scarlet lips and the dabs of rouge on her cheeks gave her the look of a sinister clown. Her dark eyes were black-rimmed and bloodshot, and Matt could see now that the glossy pyramid of hair was a wig. He wondered if she was bald underneath.

Her plump hands, adorned with several rings, pulled and twitched at the shapeless mass of black that covered her body.

"So!" she fired at them, her voice harsh and gutteral with anger. "Little busybodies! Prying and poking and sneaking around the house, listening at keyholes! So now you know everything! And now it will be all the worse for you, you nasty little nuisances!"

Sam clutched Matt's hand. Her sharp nails dug in painfully. "Please let us go. We promise we won't say anything. My parents won't tell anyone either. As long as you let us go!"

Great Aunt Dorothy laughed, a slurpy chesty laugh that set her mounds of flesh shaking in several directions at once. "What a naïve little creature it is! You expect us to believe that? No, no, it is much too late. It is all very regrettable, but now you must bear the consequences!"

"Consequences! You were going to kill us both anyway!" Matt flung at her.

"Such a shame for you, Matt. I do like little boys. If Samantha had not filled your brain with nonsense, I might have kept you as a pet! Now -" she shrugged indifferently, " - I am growing tired. There is nothing more to discuss."

"Yes there is!" said Matt. "You think I'm nothing, just a runaway, but everyone's looking for me. The people at the Home – the police – my father will have told them -"

"Your father?" Great Aunt Dorothy raised an eyebrow. "Ah yes. I think we met him."

"You – met him?" Matt echoed faintly. "How? Where?"

"Here, of course. He came to the gates. A tall man, thin with sandy hair? Very agitated. Of course, we told him we knew nothing about you."

"But – how did he know where to look?"

"It seems that a tramp had contacted him after your photograph appeared in a newspaper. He hoped for a reward, no doubt."

Matt slumped against Sam's bed. His father had been here. His father had come looking for him. He must still love him if he had started to search on his own. Tears burned his eyelids. He felt Sam give his fingers a sympathetic squeeze.

"But enough of this! Angelo!"

And Mr Higgins appeared behind Great Aunt Dorothy's wheelchair. In his hand he held a very efficient looking gun. It was pointing directly at Sam and Matt.

"Unfortunately we must keep Samantha alive until the morning, but with you, Matt, there is no such problem," said Great Aunt Dorothy. She backed her wheelchair into the corridor and Mr Higgins took her place. He gestured to Matt with the gun.

"You! Out here!"

Matt had never felt so scared in his life. His legs

wouldn't move. "You – you can't kill me," he croaked. "The police will -"

"The English police are idiots," said Mr Higgins scornfully. "They see nothing and understand nothing!". He gestured again with the gun, "I am losing patience, young man. Do you wish me to shoot you in front of your friend?"

Dragging his steps, Matt moved towards the door.

Behind him Sam screamed. "No! No! You can't kill him!"

Ignoring her Mr Higgins pulled Matt into the corridor, slammed the door and locked it. He prodded Matt roughly in the small of his back. "To your room!"

As he stumbled along the corridor, hearing Sam screaming and banging on her door, Matt felt the hairs rising on the back of his neck. How far would he get before Mr Higgins put a bullet through him? Thoughts jumbled in his brain. It would be messy to kill him here. The landing carpet was pale green. He pictured it splattered with red blood and felt sick. How far up the walls did blood splatter from a bullet wound? If anyone came to the house they would know there had been a crime. Even if you washed blood away the police could still find it using ultra violet light or something. He'd seen that on television.

But of course no-one would come. No-one would be allowed through those gates. And very soon, maybe even tomorrow, the Coopers – the real Coopers – and Sam would also be dead. Their corpses would be stowed in the crypt while the gang got away to safety.

He pictured himself in that dark place. Dead. Or maybe not properly dead, which would be worse. A sob rose in his throat and stuck there, making him gasp for breath.

They had reached Matt's room. He stood, facing the door. Now. Now it would happen. He squeezed his eyes shut and tried to control his shaking legs.

But Mr Higgins did not shoot. Instead he pushed Matt inside the room. "You may have a few more hours to say your prayers," he said, "while I make our preparations. But do not think we will let you live. I will be back before daylight."

Then the door slammed and Matt heard the sound of the key in the lock. He fell to his knees and gave way to a frenzy of sobbing.

Afterwards, exhausted, eyes hot and aching, he curled up on the bed and thought about his father, and Matron at the Home, and Mr Garner. His life hadn't been that bad, he realised now that it was almost over. Running away had been a stupid thing to do. He wondered what his father was doing now. Was he still searching? Was he still somewhere near?

But even if he was right outside the gates, there was no way in. Or out.

But there *was* a way out. The ladder! No-one knew that he had hidden it. He could scale the gates and go and fetch help. First, though, he would have to find a way out of his room.

He slipped off the bed and crept towards the door, hoping against hope that the lock might be faulty. He turned the handle as slowly and quietly as he could. Would anyone be outside the door, watching to see if he tried?

The door wouldn't open.

Next, he tried the window. The Chubb locks were as solid as ever, the double glazing looked impossible to smash, even if he could find something heavy enough to hammer it,.

He circled the room, searching and feeling for hollow sounding panels, cupboards with false backs, loose floorboards. The house was old. Surely a secret passage was possible. But he found nothing.

Dispirited, he padded over to the fireplace, sank down on to the rug and lowered his head to his clasped knees. It was no good.

There was no way out. And in a few hours he would be dead.

14

The Chimney

The sudden fall of soot made no noise as it drifted down to the hearth. Matt guessed it had been caused by nothing more than a bird settling on the chimney top, but the first tiny seed of an idea began to germinate in his brain.

Craven Manor was an old house, built in the days when logs were the only means of heating, and even in the bedrooms the fireplaces were large and functional. When Matt had arrived at the Manor he had barely registered the clusters of huge chimneys that loomed above the grey gables of the house but now he recalled them, and he remembered something else. Years ago one of his aunts had given him a book for his birthday. He hadn't bothered to read it for ages because of its soppy title, something about babies, but one day with nothing else to do he'd picked it up and found to his surprise that parts of it had been quite exciting. It had described the young boys who in those bad old days had been forced to climb the insides of chimneys to clean them, and Matt remembered the shivers of horror the tale had aroused in him, and the relief that he lived in the twenty first century and would never have to do such a thing himself.

He stared at the fireplace thoughtfully. Of course, he wasn't really considering it, he told himself. But he would just have a quick glance first. Just out of curiosity.

Crouching, he peered up the inside of the chimney and was relieved to see nothing but a dense blackness. It's bricked up, he told himself thankfully as he backed away.

But the sky itself was black. *Really* black with hardly any stars. How could he be sure that the blackness he had seen was a bricked-up blackness and not just the night sky? Well, it didn't matter anyway. He had no intention of doing such a stupid thing as climbing that chimney. What if he got stuck halfway? Or what if Mr Higgins or Irene came in and lit a fire under him? He shuddered. No. Even if being shot at dawn was the only alternative, he couldn't do it. He turned back to the bed, crawled beneath the covers, rolled himself into a ball and tried to close his mind to what was going to happen in the morning.

Five minutes passed. Ten minutes. And then ….

Oh hell! Flinging the bedclothes aside he got out and stamped across to the fireplace.

Again he peered upwards and this time he saw the faintest sparkle of light in the blackness above him,. It was a star, a single faint far-off star. So what did it prove? He argued with himself. It proved that the chimney was not blocked off. It didn't prove that it was wide enough to climb, that there would be proper footholds, that he wouldn't fall down or get stuck or – He thrust from his mind further, more gruesome, possibilities.

Climbing up the chimney was definitely not something he wanted to do, but what other choices did he have? He sighed. None.

All right, he thought. Here goes. Standing to his full

height inside the base of the chimney he stretched his hands above him and began to explore the sides. So far, so good. There was ample room for his shoulders, the broadest part of him, and the crevices between the stones were deep enough to take his fingers and the toes of his shoes. Still he hesitated. He pictured birds stuck in chimneys, dying slowly of thirst and starvation. He pictured the children in that book. No, he couldn't do it. He couldn't.

Then he took a deep breath and began to climb.

He had not been prepared for all the soot. He had expected to get dirty but he could never have imagined the thick choking blanket that began to smother him as he climbed. Every movement he made brought more soot cascading down, silting up his eyes and nose and mouth until he felt he was being buried alive. He couldn't breathe.

Panic filled him, but he managed to turn his face downwards and draw a single vile-tasting breath. Then he willed himself to remain motionless, eyes and lips tightly closed, lungs bursting, until the soot gradually settled.

Cautiously he took another deep breath, held it, and climbed another few inches, fingers and feet groping for crevices. The soot swirled again and he waited again, then moved upwards a little further. It was tiring work and panic kept threatening to overwhelm him but he was winning, he told himself. The constant pauses made progress slow but he thought he must be halfway by now, perhaps on a level with the ceiling of his bedroom. There was still the shaft that went up through the top floor of the house, the attic floor, but after that he would be within a few feet of the opening.

And then he slipped. The notch into which he had wedged his right foot suddenly crumbled, his fingers lost their grip and he was plunging down through the blackness, chin, wrists, elbows and knees painfully scraping against the old stones. He didn't fall all the way to the bottom. His fall ended with a few final agonising scrapes and he found himself wedged, still upright but with one knee jammed against his stomach and his left sleeve caught on some small projection above his head. The soot swirled in a dense cloud and the inside of his mouth was caked with the stuff. His lungs were empty, the air knocked out of them by his fall, and panic-stricken he wanted to snatch mouthfuls of the thick black atmosphere around him, like a drowning man gulps water. But somehow he forced himself to wait until the soot settled.

At last he found he was able to breathe. But he hurt all over. He could feel tears welling up in his eyes and forcing muddy paths down his cheeks and his nose began to bubble like a baby's. If he ever got out of this, he sobbed, he would never do anything stupid again but please, let this all be over by the time he had counted to a thousand.

It was a silly prayer but the counting helped to keep him calm when he discovered that he could not go down the last few feet of the chimney. His jammed knee meant that the only way he could go was up, and that only by strenuous heaving and pushing, but once he started again he determined that he would reach the top or die in the attempt.

He climbed more quickly this time, his hands and feet

more confident and practised, and soon he was beyond the point where he had fallen. But then he encountered another problem: the chimney began to narrow as it passed through the attics. He struggled on, the walls of the shaft pressing more and more uncomfortably against his body, his movements restricted to mere wriggles. He stopped, held in position by the jailer's grip of the chimney, and felt fear rising up in him again. How much narrower would it become? Would it reach the point where he was well and truly stuck, unable to go on or retreat? He thought of dying in this narrow black prison and he imagined his body lodged for years, perhaps even centuries, no-one knowing he was there. Unless someone tried to light a fire.

He still had a choice. He could go on. It was a risk, a terrible risk, but he was so near success. Already he could feel cooler fresher air above him and the burnt sooty smell of the walls was less noticeable. Or he could go back. And at this thought his heart sank.

If he went back all his efforts would have been wasted, all his scrapes and bruises in vain. And then he would have to face the morning and a bullet from Mr Higgins' gun. No, there was no choice. He had to go on.

For once he was thankful that he was small for his age and he tried to make himself even smaller, stretching his arms high above his head and folding in his shoulders to lessen their width. It was a struggle but determinedly he pushed and squeezed, propelled only by the upward thrust of his feet. His legs ached and he ascended by slow agonising inches but he was moving, coming closer and closer to freedom, until at last he felt the play of cool air on his face. The top of his head was level with the top of the chimney.

He paused and rested for a moment. Then he braced his legs and gave one last tremendous desperate heave. For a moment he stuck and then, like a cork popping out of a bottle of champagne, his head and shoulders shot upwards and he half fell, half collapsed, over the brick stack.

He had done it! For a long moment he rested, legs still dangling inside the chimney while he took gulps of the fresh night air. Then he summoned one last effort and hauled himself out on to the roof.

15

Over the Wall

The climb had taken a long time and Matt lay spreadeagled across the ridge of the roof, his whole body trembling with exhaustion.

The night sky was a little brighter now. The trees and shrubs below showed as varying tones of grey and from above he could see the ruins of the Abbey, and quite a distance beyond, the gravel drive and the gates.

He raised his head cautiously, watching and listening for movement, but the world below seemed asleep.

An ordeal still lay ahead of him. He had to get down to the ground, and the ground was a sickening twelve metres or more below him. The roof was steep, the tiles old and worn and, he guessed, easily dislodged.

He began the descent, edging crabwise down the steep slope, clinging with fingers and toes for any foothold. He found he was holding his breath, biting painfully into his lower lip. He could taste the salt of blood in his mouth.

It was going well until a tile moved beneath his feet, and then he was slipping and sliding down towards the roof edge, arms flailing as he fought to keep his balance and stop his fall. But instead he gained momentum, and in his terror he found himself yelling.

And then he was hanging over the edge, clinging by his fingers to a gutter that creaked ominously. He hung there for long minutes, groping with his feet for something to support his body before his arms gave way. One foot found something, a window ledge or a parapet, and he was able to adjust his weight and release one hand to search for another hold.

With a shaky prayer of thanks he found a drainpipe within reach. Maybe it wouldn't take his weight but he had to try. He waited, trying to control his shaking and summon up some energy, and then he threw himself towards the drainpipe and wrapped himself around it.

He had made so much noise he expected to see lights appearing all over the house and in the grounds below, but thankfully all seemed quiet.

Slowly and as silently as he could, he lowered himself down the drainpipe until at last he felt firm ground beneath his feet. There he waited, ears pricked for any sound or movement from the house or grounds, but nothing stirred and the only sound was the mournful hoot of an owl in the trees.

He crept towards the clump of evergreens where he had hidden the ladder. He had that feeling in the back of his neck that someone was watching him, but he had to hope it was just his imagination.

When he reached the ladder he hesitated. What about the Coopers? If he made for the Abbey he reckoned he might be able to break the trapdoor padlock with a stone and release them from the Crypt. Then it would be three against five. But hammering with just a stone would take time and make a noise. Mr Higgins and his gang might come to investigate and they had weapons. He stood indecisively. As for Sam – if he could get back into the house he might be able to let her out. But Sam would be a hindrance, not a help. She was impulsive and he doubted that she could do anything quietly. No, although he felt guilty at abandoning her, he knew he would be faster on his own, and once he was outside the grounds he would try to find a house with a telephone and raise the alarm. He just hoped someone would believe him.

He pulled out the ladder from behind the shrubs. It seemed even heavier now that he was so exhausted but he gritted his teeth and began the long walk to the gates.

It was still too dark to read the time on his watch but he guessed it must be around three in the morning. There might be only two or three hours before Mr Higgins looked for him in his bedroom. Despite his tiredness and the weight of the ladder he must move faster.

It seemed an eternity but at last he reached the gates. The ladder was one of those complicated multi-position contraptions and Matt tugged and cursed for some time before he had it unfolded and propped against the gates.

He heaved a huge sigh. Just a handful of rungs to climb and he would be free.

He was just halfway up the ladder when he heard the rush of footsteps along the drive. His heart started to hammer. Risking a glance behind him, he saw Mr Higgins and the fake Mr Cooper only four or five metres away. Both were holding revolvers.

This was it. His last chance.

Galvanised into action he scrabbled up the last few rungs of the ladder, grabbed the top of the gates and flung himself over, hearing the whistle of a bullet just inches from his head.

He landed with a bone-shattering thump. Sharp stones dug into his hands and knees but he ignored them, and as the gates began to swing open he ran for the dark shelter of the woods.

Behind him he heard the two men swearing as they crashed through the trees, but he didn't dare risk another backward glance. A second bullet whistled past him and full of a new terrified energy he ran as he had never run before. Gradually the voices died away, until around him he heard only the thud of his own feet and the rustle of birds and animals disturbed by his progress.

He had no idea where he was, but he tried to run in a straight line, hoping that eventually he would come to a road or a village. On and on he ran, his blood racing in his veins, his breathing a painful rasp in his throat. Branches tore at his face and arms but he ignored them. The adrenalin of fear had swept away his fatigue and he felt he could run forever now. Nothing mattered except to find help.

And then he heard the voices of men and the sound of feet ahead of him. His heart sank. Mr Higgins and Mr Cooper. He must have been running in a circle, and now he was about to be caught. He pressed himself against the broad trunk of an oak tree and tried to control his harsh breathing.

But as the voices grew louder he realised that they were not the voices of Mr Higgins and Mr Cooper. There were more of them, three at least.

And one of them was familiar. More than familiar.

"Dad?" he croaked. "DAD?"

"Matt? Oh God, where are you?"

"Here! I'm here!"

Matt stumbled forward, and into the arms of his father.

16

Dad

His father clutched him as if he would never again let him go. "We've been searching for you since yesterday morning," he said. He jerked his head towards the other two men, who were standing behind him with broad grins on their faces. "My mates Dave and Nick have been helping me."

"What about the police? Are they here too?"

"They sent out some men yesterday during daylight hours but then they pulled them back, said it was too dark to continue. So I phoned Dave and Nick and they came out like a shot. I'm really grateful to them."

"You've been searching all night?" Matt swallowed a huge lump in his throat. "How did you know where to look?"

"A tramp contacted me through the radio station, said he'd met you and given you breakfast."

"He stole all my money!" said Matt bitterly.

"*Did* he? And I gave him £25 for the information!" Mr Bright shook his head. "Well, at least he set us on the right track. But then I found your mobile phone and that set us off in the wrong direction. We've been going round in circles for hours. I called at some large house beyond these woods, but they hadn't seen you -"

"They lied to you. That's where I've been. That's where I escaped from!"

"Escaped!"

"Dad, I can't tell you everything right now but things are really bad. We have to get the police here. The gang in there are going to kill my friend and her parents. We don't have long. Days – maybe even hours!"

Mr Bright stared at him, his jaw dropping. "You're not really serious, are you, son?"

"Absolutely serious. We have to get the police and convince them."

Mr Bright was quiet.

"It's true, Dad. Honestly."

"Matt. Matt. You don't have to make up stories, you know. You're not going to get into trouble."

"Dad, on my word of honour it's true! I wouldn't lie about it. That's why I had to escape. And if we don't hurry it'll be too late!"

"Well, I guess I'll have to believe you, if you swear it's the truth, but I'm not sure the police will, you have to admit it sounds pretty far fetched."

"It's true!" Matt insisted.

Mr Bright sighed. "Well, I wouldn't want anyone's death on my conscience, so here goes!" He pulled out his phone and dialled 999.

Matt listened as his father told the police about his son's imprisonment and the threat to the family at Craven Manor. He could tell that his father was finding it difficult to convince them, but eventually they arranged to meet at a crossroads near the Manor.

"I'm not sure they believed me," said Mr Bright after he ended the call. "But they're bound to investigate. Now, let's get back to my car." He turned to his friends. "Dave, Nick – there's no point in you hanging around as well. I'll see you both tomorrow. But thanks, guys, for all your help. I'm really in your debt."

At the crossroads Matt waited with his father for what seemed like an age. He fidgeted and checked his watch over and over as dawn brightened the sky.

"Where are they?" he muttered.

A police car arrived at the meeting place at six thirty. Inside were an inspector and his female sergeant.

"Where are the rest of you?" Matt demanded as they got out of the car.

"The rest? There's just us, Sonny," said the Inspector.

"But they've got guns – two of you won't be enough," said Matt.

"Oh, I think we'll manage," said the Inspector.

"You don't believe me, do you?"

The Inspector turned to Mr Bright. "I'm glad you've got your son back," he said, "but I think he's been taken in by the young lady who lives at the Manor. We've had this story before, you know, but I met the Coopers a few weeks ago. There's no doubt they're the girl's parents."

"You're wrong!" said Matt. "They're look-alikes. The real Coopers are locked up in the crypt below the Abbey – and if you don't rescue them now, they'll die! Sam too. I only managed to escape because I climbed up a chimney."

The Inspector looked sceptical. "I can see you're covered in soot, but - "

"I don't think my son's lying," said Mr Bright. "If he says they're in danger, then that's the truth."

The Inspector hesitated. "All right," he said to Matt. "Tell me the whole story and I'll decide what to do."

Matt was very conscious of the minutes passing as he

gabbled out at high speed the events of the past few days and told of the conversations he had overheard. By the time he finished it was past seven and the morning was bright.

"Please! They're planning to kill them as soon as they get the formula. It may already be too late!"

The Inspector still hesitated and Matt, his father and the two other men waited for his decision.

"All right," he said at last and turned to his sergeant. "Radio for some assistance," he told her.

"What about guns?" asked Matt.

"Sonny, you've been watching too much television," sad the Inspector. "We don't use arms except as a last resort."

Matt glared at the man's complacent face and hated him.

The assistance came at last. Another patrol car, two policemen inside.

They drove in convoy to the gates of the Manor, Mr Bright's car at the rear. It was now nearly eight thirty and Matt couldn't get rid of the horrible feeling that Mr Higgins and his gang would be gone and all they would find would be dead bodies.

There was a long wait after the Inspector pressed the entry buttons, but just as Matt was about to demand they break the gates down, they opened and Mr Higgins appeared.

"Inspector Ryder! We meet again!" His eyes glanced over the other man's shoulder and saw the gathering of police, Mr Bright and his friends and, lastly, Matt. He smiled his full-lipped smile. "But what a coincidence. I was just about to call you."

"Oh yes?"

"Yes indeed. To report the disappearance of that young man there, but I see you have already found him. Well done!"

Mr Bright stepped forward. "If you remember, I called on you yesterday. This is my son. You told me you knew nothing about him!"

"But I assure you, I did not. This young man was introduced to us as Matt Jackson, not Bright. My pupil, Samantha, told us he was a school friend."

"Is this true?" the Inspector asked Matt.

"Yes, but -"

The Inspector sighed . "All the same, Mr Higgins, there have been serious allegations and I am duty bound to follow them up. May we see Mr and Mrs Cooper and their daughter Samantha, please?"

"But of course, Inspector. We have nothing to hide." Mr Higgins stepped back and gestured the police to follow him.

They found the fake Coopers and Sam inside the drawing room.

"Matt! Look at you!" Sam gasped.

He had forgotten the coating of soot that covered him from head to foot He brushed at it half heartedly, sending drifts to the carpet. He looked around. The Coopers were standing by the fireside, with an expression of concern on their faces. The table at their side was set with delicate china cups and a cafetiere of coffee. It looked like any normal breakfast scene, except for Sam, who sat by the window, looking pale and tense. There was no sign of Irene. Had she been sent to take care of Sam's parents?

Inspector Ryder was explaining his visit to the fake Coopers. Mrs Cooper sighed and shook her head. "Poor Matt," she said. "I'm afraid Sam has been filling his head with nonsense. Of course, she and her friends read all these Gothic novels nowadays."

"Where's Irene?" demanded Matt.

"She has a day off. Her mother is ill."

I bet she hasn't even *got* a mother, thought Matt. She was with the real Coopers, he knew it.

"You locked me in!" he accused Mr Higgins.

Mr Higgins laughed. "Matt, Matt! You were never locked in. You know how heavy the doors are in such an old building. No, no, you were never locked in."

"Sam! Tell them!" said Matt. "Tell them what's been happening!"

Sam stared at him, her eyes wide and dark in her pale face. "Nothing," she said. "Nothing's been happening." Her voice was dull. "I was just – playing games with you."

"You see?" said Mr Higgins. "It is all a nonsense."

"She's lying! Tell them, Sam!"

But she was silent.

"Sam's behaviour has caused us a lot of embarrassment, Inspector," said Mr Cooper. "I'm sure you will remember from your previous visit how much she delights in these -" He waved a pale languid hand - "How shall I describe them? I think perhaps she read the Grimms Brothers fairy tales at too tender an age! I am so very sorry that you've been called out again all for nothing."

"Perhaps we can offer you and your men some tea or coffee before you go," suggested Mrs Cooper.

Matt watched Sam. Something was wrong. He could see how tense she was. Her hands twisted and clenched, her fingernails drawing blood here and there. Her eyes avoided his. She was frightened. Mr Higgins must have said something bad would happen if she said anything, something even worse than the threat that already hung over her. But what could be worse? Torture? A more violent and gruesome death than shooting?

"Well, I apologise for bothering you, and so early in the morning," the Inspector was saying. "You do understand that we have to investigate when we receive a complaint." He turned to Sam. "You've taken up a lot of police time one way or another, young lady, and while we've been wasting time here someone else might have been in *real* trouble."

Sam lowered her eyes. "I'm sorry," she muttered.

Matt willed her to look at him. If she didn't say anything now, he knew it would be too late. Perhaps she thought she was protecting her parents, but he knew that any promises Mr Higgins had made to her were meaningless. She and the real Coopers would be killed as soon as the police were gone.

"Sam! Sam!" he hissed. "Say something."

But Sam, still refusing to meet his eyes, moved across to the fake Coopers and stood beside them, her hand resting on Mrs Cooper's shoulder.

Don't do this, he pleaded with her silently. This is your last chance. Tell the police what's been happening"

"Thanks for the offer of tea, sir," said the Inspector, "but we have to get back to the Station." He gave Sam a stern look. "As for you, miss. No more fairy tales, eh? Come on, young Matt. I think we need to have a little talk."

"No, wait! I know what I saw and heard. The real Coopers are prisoners and I can prove it. I'll show you the way into the crypt -"

"Now, now, son. The matter is closed."

"But I can show you - "

The Inspector gripped Matt's arm. "Come along now. We'll let these good people have their breakfast in peace."

Matt gave Sam one last imploring look and then, sick at heart, he found himself outside the house, being escorted down the drive and through the gates.

17

Mr Higgins Lies

Outside, Matt turned angrily to the Inspector.

"If you'd bothered to search the crypt you'd have found the real Coopers. If they die it will be your fault!"

"We can't search a property without a warrant," said the Inspector. "To get a warrant we need evidence – and there *is* no evidence. The owners told a convincing story and the girl herself admitted she was making it up -"

"She was scared. Besides, I gave you evidence. I'm a witness. I heard their plans and I saw them sneaking into the crypt. What more do you want?"

"It's your word against theirs, sonny."

"I don't think my boy was lying," said Matt's Dad.

"I'm not suggesting he's telling deliberate lies," said the Inspector. "But I do think the girl is lying – and I think Matt here has misinterpreted some of the circumstances."

"Please, *please*," said Matt. "If we could just sneak back in – get a ladder and climb over the wall – you'd see -"

The Inspector shrugged. "My hands are tied. There are certain procedures and I can't go against them. But if you find new evidence, I'll look at the situation again."

"It'll be too late by then," said Matt bitterly.

His father squeezed his shoulder. "Come on, son, let's get you back. You've done all you can."

At the Home Mrs Doherty and Mr Garner were waiting outside the front door. Mrs Doherty smothered him in a huge hug. "The police phoned and told us you'd been found," she said. "We were so worried and we're so glad to have you back."

Matt turned to his father. "You can't leave me here again. Can't I come home with you?"

"Matt, you know I've only got one room, it's just not possible."

So it had all been for nothing. Matt's eyes stung with angry tears. "I'll run away again. And next time you won't find me!"

"Please, Matt. Don't do anything stupid. Just give me a little time -"

"Time to clear off to the States!" Matt flung at him.

"No, I – that was a crazy idea, I was just feeling desperate. Look, let me see what I can do. If you'll just stay here for a little longer …. Will you promise me?"

Matt turned away. Mrs Doherty gave him an encouraging smile.

"Maybe," he muttered at last.

"I'm coming to see you next Saturday," said his father. "I promise." He stared at Matt and then pulled him into his arms. "I do love you, you know. More than anything."

After he had gone, Matt paced the rooms and corridors of the Home like a caged animal, useless ideas chasing each other through his brain. He could escape again – getting out of the Home unnoticed was easy enough – but Craven Manor was hours away. Unless he could hitch a lift all the way there he could still be too late. And once there, how would he get in? He could pester that police inspector again, but that would just make him more obstinate. He could tell his story to the newspapers, but why would they believe an eleven year old boy without any proof?

The other boys and girls were all at school and the Home was quiet, but the chimes of the grandfather clock in the hall each quarter hour were like hammer blows in his head. Each chime brought the deaths of Sam and her parents closer. If they had not already been killed.

"Matt." Mrs Doherty had appeared in the doorway, concern on her round motherly face. "You mustn't stress yourself like this. Your Dad will be here again soon. Come and have some lunch, there's a good lad."

She didn't understand. She had no idea, none of them did.

It must be nearly eighteen hours since he had last eaten, but the thought of food made him sick. "I'm not hungry," he said.

"Well, when you're ready," she sighed. "Come into the kitchen and I'll get you something."

Another hour passed, and then faintly he heard the ring of the telephone. Mrs Doherty appeared again, potato peeler in one hand, telephone in the other.

"Someone for you, Matt."

Dad, he supposed. Or perhaps someone from Social Services to lecture him.

"Hello," he grunted.

"Matt!" The voice was a whisper but he knew at once who it was. A huge wave of relief raced through his body.

"Sam! Where are you? Are you ok? How did you get to a phone? How did you know where to find me?"

"I'm in my attic. I stole Irene's mobile from her handbag, and I remembered the name of your Home from the radio."

"You – are you alright? And - " He hardly liked to ask. "Your Mum and Dad?"

"We're ok, but you have to help. You have to -"

"Wait! Wait! I've got an idea." Matt rushed to the kitchen, where Mrs Doherty and Mr Garner were seated at the kitchen table, companionably preparing vegetables for the evening meal.

Matt put the phone on Loudspeaker and waved it at them. "You have to listen to this!" he yelled. "It's my proof!"

"Proof?" asked Mr Garner. "What proof? What are you talking about?"

"Never mind. Just listen – please. Listen carefully and remember."

"But – what -"

"Sssh!" Matt yelled. "No, not you, Sam. Sam, I've asked the people here to listen to you and then they can back me up with the police -"

"Police?" asked a baffled Mrs Doherty.

"Sam, just tell us what's happening."

"I'm sorry I couldn't say anything when the police were here, Matt. Mr Higgins said they – they would set fire to the crypt – with Mummy and Daddy down there – if I breathed a word. I couldn't take the risk."

"But – you're still alive. I thought -"

"Yes, but it's all so horrible here, Matt. Everybody's angry. I heard Mr Higgins telling Irene that my parents won't finish the tests unless I'm sent to a safe place first. And Mr Higgins told *them* that he'd take me down and shoot me in front of them if they didn't do what they were told. Matt, I'm so scared. You've got to get help!"

"I will, I promise. Give me the number of the mobile so I can keep in touch with you."

"No, I'll have to sneak it back into Irene's bag, otherwise they might guess I've used it."

"All right. I'm going now, but we'll get the police and soon you'll all be safe. I promise."

Matt knew he might not be able to keep that promise, but Sam needed to stay calm.

He turned to a shocked Mr Garner. "I can't explain it all now, there isn't time, but you both heard Sam. She and her Mum and Dad are going to be killed if we don't do something to stop it. Will you phone the police and back me up?"

"Well -" Mrs Doherty rose uncertainly. "I suppose we can tell them what we heard. But it sounds like something out of a – a detective story. Are you sure?"

"It really is a matter of life or death," urged Matt. "I swear it!"

It was another hour before the information got through to Inspector Ryder and yet another hour before he was persuaded to take further action.

"I'm still not one hundred percent convinced," he grumbled. " I'd be a lot happier if I had some concrete evidence – it's a serious matter invading someone's property without it."

"But we all heard the young lady -" said Mrs Doherty.

"She seemed genuinely frightened."

"Yes, yes," he said. "But young Samantha is an expert at playing games. I've heard it all before, as Matt here knows." He rubbed his hand over a tired face. "I've three other cases on the go," he said. "All of them important, and all with evidence building up. I don't want to get egg on my face over an imaginary kidnapping."

Matt held his breath.

"Ah well," said the Inspector at last. "I suppose I'll have to risk it. On the grounds that it just might be true!"

"Can – can I come with you?"

"Oh no! Definitely not, young man. More than my job's worth. No, no, you stay right here. I'll telephone when we've investigated."

He turned back at the door. "I mean it, Matt. Stay here. No more phone calls. No more interference. You hear me?"

Matt nodded his head, but after the Inspector had gone he clutched Mr Garner by the arm. "I have to be there!"

"No, Matt, you heard what he said."

"But it could all go wrong! They might need me."

"I'm sure the Inspector will sort it."

"He didn't last time. Please, Mr Garner, you could drive me. We don't have to go inside. Just so that I'm near. *Please*, Mr Garner. We can park outside the gates. I'll stay inside the car. I promise!" At that moment Matt would have promised anything.

Eventually Mr Garner gave in. "All right, but we stay outside the gates."

Mr Garner drove his old Volvo so fast that they reached the Manor as Inspector Ryder was still marshalling his troops outside the gates.

Matt wound down his window. "I'm here if you need

me!" he called in a loud whisper.

The Inspector strode across to the car. "At this moment you're the last thing I need!" he hissed. "You're just an added worry! As for you, Mr Garner – you ought to know better!"

Mr Garner shrank back into his seat. "Sorry!"

The Inspector poked his finger at Matt. "You stay in this car and you don't move a muscle until we come out again! You hear?"

"I hear," Matt answered meekly. He watched as the Inspector pressed the intercom button on the gates.

"You're not going to warn them, are you?" he asked.

"We still can't force our way in with all guns blazing, young man. This isn't James Bond, you know."

Matt glanced at the Inspector and his sergeant and turned round to look at the following car that held two constables. "I can see that."

"No need for sarcasm, sonny!"

There was a delay of several minutes before the gates opened. Filled with dread, Matt wondered if at that very moment Sam and her parents were being murdered and the evidence destroyed.

"Now stay there until I say different!" Inspector Ryder ordered sternly. "You promise?"

He had no intention of keeping that promise. He waited until the second car had followed the Inspector's and then, just as the gates started to close he flung open his door and raced through the narrowing gap, ignoring the anxious cry from Mr Garner.

18

The Arrest

Under cover of the Manor garden's plentiful shrubs he reached the front door unseen. The door was closed. The police were all inside. He crept round to the back of the house and down the stone steps to the basement room where he had found the ladder, praying that the outside door was still unlocked. It was. Holding his breath he lifted the latch.

Upstairs he followed the murmur of voices to the drawing room. The door was slightly ajar. The Coopers, Mr Higgins, Sam and the four police were grouped by the fireplace. No sign of Irene. Or Great Aunt Dorothy. Matt crouched down and crept into the shelter of one of the room's large sofas.

Mr Higgins was speaking. As usual he had taken the lead.

"Another wasted visit, Inspector! You say Samantha telephoned young Matthew. But you know already how that young girl fantasizes." He crossed to Mrs Cooper and laid a sympathetic hand on her shoulder. "Poor Mrs Cooper – and Mr Cooper too. Such a burden for them. They have tried so hard to keep it quiet – it is obviously not something they would wish to have known – but their daughter, Samantha, is a schizophrenic. It is most unfortunate, but we are dealing with it. She sees a consultant monthly in London, and of course she is under medication." Mr Higgins sighed. "But sometimes, I am afraid, the medication becomes ineffective and she hears her voices again -"

"Is this true, Mrs Cooper?" asked the Inspector.

"It is, Inspector," said the fake Mrs Cooper. "It's a terrible illness. We try to help Samantha all we can, but it's not easy."

Matt waited for Sam to protest but she said nothing. He risked a peep around the arm of the sofa and his heart sank. Her face was white and her lips a tight trembling line. It was obvious that she was under threat again.

But he had to make her speak. Staying silent wouldn't save her or her parents. Once the police left, the gang were free again to do whatever they wanted. At best Sam was providing another hour or so of life before the three of them were murdered.

"Well, Samantha?" asked Inspector Ryder. "What do you have to say?"

"I'm sorry," she whispered.

Matt couldn't wait any longer. He sprang to his feet.

"Sam! Tell them! Tell them the truth! It's the only way you can save them!"

All eyes turned to him and it seemed that everyone in the room froze in disbelief.

"Whatever they've threatened you with – whatever they've promised – you know you can't trust them. Once we've gone you'll be killed. You know it! Please, Sam," he urged. "The police won't come back a third time. You have to tell them now!"

Sam's eyes, wide with fear, travelled from one face to another.

"All right," she whispered, and half rose from her

chair.

Then two things happened at once. Mr Higgins began to draw a mobile from his pocket and Sam screamed.

"Don't let him use the phone! He's going to signal Irene -"

Matt waited for no more. He threw himself at Mr Higgins and knocked the phone to the floor, and then he stamped on it until it was in the smallest of pieces.

"Why, you -" Mr Higgins' eyes were murderous as he lunged for Matt's throat, but his lunge was cut short by the sergeant, who had him in handcuffs within seconds.

The Inspector stared coldly at Mr Higgins. "I think we will investigate after all," he said. "And for the time being at least, you're all under arrest!"

"There's another of them upstairs," said Sam quickly. "She's in a wheelchair."

The Inspector nodded to two of his men "Bring her down." He turned to Matt. "Now, Sonny. Let's see what's in that crypt."

"Irene's there," said Sam. "She's got a gun. She had orders to – to shoot my parents if Mr Higgins -"

"There, there," soothed the Inspector's sergeant. "We're here now. Nothing bad is going to happen."

Matt hoped she was right.

"I know it's round here somewhere," said Matt.

They had been searching the grounds around the ruins of the Abbey for twenty minutes. Matt, the Inspector, his sergeant and one of the policemen. Sam had wanted to come with them but the Inspector had forbidden it, and Matt was glad she wasn't there. Who knew what they might find?

"You're absolutely sure about this?" asked the Inspector. He was growing impatient.

"I'm sure. It's a trapdoor. I saw them opening it. There were lots of stones around it, and weeds and other stuff -"

"Sir!" The sergeant was pulling away mounds of grass, weeds and twigs. The trapdoor had been well hidden.

The Inspector pulled out the key he had demanded from Mr Higgins and inserted it into the smoothly oiled padlock.

"Police!" he called as he raised the trapdoor. "We're coming in. Put down your weapon!"

But Irene, standing at the foot of the wooden steps, still held the gun. She pointed it unsteadily at the Inspector as he climbed down, followed by the sergeant.

"Don't be a fool," he told her. "You can't get away. Your accomplices have all been arrested."

Slowly Irene handed him the gun and turned to lead the way into the crypt. It had been fitted out as a laboratory, with benches, Bunsen burners, a microscope and all the paraphernalia for scientific experiments. Brilliantly lit tanks held a collection of plants and other lights had been rigged to shine on to the benches, but the outer boundaries of the crypt were in darkness.

Where were the Coopers?

And then Matt heard a moan. It came from behind one of the stone pillars.

"They're here!" he yelled.

And there they were. Bound and gagged, but alive.

Their first thought after they were released was for Sam.

"She's fine," said Matt. "Waiting to see you."

Back at the Manor all the gang including Great Aunt Dorothy were in the sitting room, handcuffed and under guard.

Sam burst into tears and flew to her parents. "I thought I'd never see you again!"

"It's all right, darling," said Mrs Cooper, gathering her into her arms. "Sssh now, everything's all right."

The Inspector's bemused gaze moved between the real and the fake Coopers. "Well! It's easy to see how we were all taken in. I've never seen such a resemblance!"

Sam glared at him. "*I* wasn't taken in, not for a minute – but none of you would believe me!"

The Inspector nodded "Then I owe you an apology, young lady." He turned to Sam's parents. "Perhaps you can tell us what's been going on."

And while one of the constables went to the kitchen to make cups of tea the Coopers began their story.

"We were searching for new plant specimens in the Brazilian rain forest," said Mr Cooper. "We hadn't intended to travel quite so far but the results had been a little disappointing so we kept going, and eventually we came to an area that I don't think had been explored before. We came across a group of people, a small tribe, who seemed to be extraordinarily healthy and disease-free. It seemed too that they lived to an exceptional age, well over 100 in most cases."

"Of course, they didn't have calendars or written

records," said Mr Cooper, "and we were communicating partly in sign language, but everything seemed to bear out what we saw."

It appeared that they relied upon a plant which grew only in their part of the forest and had special qualities that their ancestors had known of for centuries. "And then we learned something else," he went on. "It seemed that the plant could reverse the effects of damage to the body brought on by injury or food poisoning or any form of stress. We did see one or two examples and they seemed quite miraculous. It's really quite difficult to describe how it worked – I think the best I can do is to compare it with System Restore on a computer – of course, they didn't have computers either!

"Anyway," he went on, "After a lot of persuasion and in exchange for all sorts of gifts – everything from perfume to penknives, a mobile phone (useless in the forest of course!), a pair of my boots, even a couple of locks of my wife's red hair! - they gave us some specimens of the plant."

On their return to Rio de Janeiro the Coopers found that rumours were already circulating about their find, and it was not long before Mr Higgins (whose real name, they told the Inspector, was Angelo Garcia) contacted them. They believed he was a reporter for the Correio do Brasil, a local newspaper, and gave him an interview.

"The interview never appeared in the newspaper, but a week later Garcia came to see us again," said Mr Cooper. "He told us that one of his colleagues in England had Sam under surveillance, and if we didn't do exactly as we were told, something would happen to her."

"We didn't dare go to the police," said Mrs Cooper. She pulled Sam closer. "He was such a hard cold man, we knew he wouldn't hesitate to get her killed."

"Anyway," Mr Cooper carried on, "he forced us to write to our staff dismissing them, and then we had to come back to England. Garcia and his mother came with us." He stared at Great Aunt Dorothy with dislike. "I think she was the brains behind the whole plan!"

"Once we got here we were bundled into the crypt. It seems Garcia's accomplice had spent several days here at the Manor and had discovered the passage leading to it. He and Garcia decided it was the ideal place to keep us prisoner. They smuggled all the equipment down there before they brought Sam home."

Mr Cooper hesitated and looked across at Sam. "They let me see her once or twice, just to prove they were keeping her alive. They handcuffed and gagged me, then brought me up to the surface." Sam gasped. He smiled at her. "I saw you riding. You've improved a lot. More rosettes in the offing!"

The Inspector nodded his head towards the fake Coopers. "What about these two?" he asked.

"Garcia hired them to impersonate us. It meant they could visit the bank and other places in the area without raising suspicion. They took our credit cards and other documents. I expect they've faked our signatures and drawn out quite a lot of money already."

"We had nothing to do with all this," interrupted the fake Mr Cooper. "We're just actors, we were hired to do a job. *He* told us it was just a bit of fun!"

"That's not true," said Matt. "They knew everything, they were there when the others were planning to kill us!"

"Actors!" sneered Garcia. "Has-beens! Neither of you had worked for years. If I had not found your photographs on the Internet and seen the resemblance you would still be cleaning restrooms or stacking shelves in a supermarket! I have paid you well and you knew exactly what would happen."

"And you?" asked the Inspector, pointing at Irene. "Who exactly are you?"

"I'm just the housekeeper," Irene said quickly. "But he forced me to guard the Coopers."

Great Aunt Dorothy gave a contemptuous snort. "Housekeeper! She's my son's wife – not of *my* choice, I can tell you! A dancer in a nightclub! It is she who wanted the Coopers' money." She wriggled her plump hands. "Greedy, greedy, greedy! Grab, grab, grab!"

"But it's you who wanted the drug," said Irene.

"There is no drug," said Mr Cooper.

"Of course there is a drug," said Great Aunt Dorothy. "You have been working on it for nearly two months. Of course there is a drug."

Mr Cooper shook his head. "They gave us the wrong plants. They didn't want us to have their secrets, but I also think the tribe in the rain forest had inherited very healthy genes and the plants just gave them an extra boost. All the time you kept us in that crypt we've known. We grew the plants on and did the tests, but only to buy time for our daughter's sake."

Great Aunt Dorothy's face drained of blood. "No – o – o – o!" she screamed. "I need that drug. I need it!" Her huge body seemed to crumple in the wheelchair as if air were being let out of a balloon and her breath came in heavy gulps. "I need it!"

Mr Cooper stared at her coldly. "Well, you'll never get it, and I'm glad. You were prepared to kill us, kill my daughter, kill this boy, just so that you could be given an easy way to undo all the harm you've done to your body. I'm glad we failed."

19

Happy Families

As soon as the Inspector and his team had taken away the prisoners Sam flew across the room and to Matt's huge embarrassment flung her arms around his neck and gave him a big kiss on the mouth.

"You saved us!" she said.

Matt squirmed. "It was nothing."

"It was a great deal," said Mrs Cooper. "We must do something to repay you, Matt."

"He could stay with us, couldn't he, Mummy?" said Sam. "Then he wouldn't have to go back to that horrible old Home!"

Mrs Cooper paused. "Well, I -"

"I've just remembered," said Matt quickly. "I left Mr Garner outside the gates. I'd better go." The Coopers didn't want him. Why should they? Nobody wanted him really. Not even his Dad, who had worried enough to come searching for him but still didn't want him in his life.

"Of course. But we'd love to have you here for a holiday, Matt – or perhaps you could even come abroad with us sometime. Would you like that?"

Matt nodded and tried to smile.

"You will come, won't you, Matt?" Sam asked urgently. "Promise?"

He looked at her. They were poles apart, they had nothing in common, and Sam seemed a different person now, the sharp corners of her face softened with happiness. She had her real parents back and it was clear as anything how much they loved her. He envied her. Perhaps they would keep in touch but she would never really need him again. Nobody needed him.

Over the next few days everyone at the Home fussed over him. Everyone wanted to be his friend. News of the events at Craven Manor had got out and reporters and cameramen hung around the Home, ringing the doorbells, trampling the flower beds in the garden and generally being a nuisance. Only the appearance of Mrs Doherty, a flying red faced fury at the front door, could scare them away.

Sam had phoned on his first day back. She tried to persuade Matt to come for a weekend but he refused. There was only one thing he wanted now, to be back home with his father. And that wasn't going to happen.

He wondered if he should run away again. But what was the point? What had he gained last time? Nothing had changed. He was still in the home. His Dad still didn't want him.

"Cheer up, Mattie, you're a hero!" said Mrs Doherty.

But nothing could cheer him. Maybe he should ask her to tell his Dad not to come on Saturday. Show him that Matt didn't want *him*.

The days passed slowly and miserably but at last it was Saturday and he couldn't help a stirring of hope. Then Mrs Doherty was calling up the stairs.

"Your Dad just phoned, Mattie." His heart plunged. *He's not coming,* he thought drearily.

"Just to let you know he's taking you out. That Mr and Mrs Cooper have asked to see you." Mrs Doherty appeared on the landing. "Now come on, darling. Let's get you tidied up. Look at your hair! Sticking up like a duck's ar – backside! And that tee shirt, only fit for the dustbin! Come and put your good clothes on."

He submitted to her fussing and smoothing. What did it matter? Nevertheless, as the time drew near he returned to the landing window again and again to watch for his father's car turning into the road.

And just before noon it came. He watched as his father got out, went round to the passenger door and opened it. He had brought Samantha.

She stepped out of the car and looked up at the landing window as if sensing Matt's gaze. She waved vigorously and then they were inside the house and his father was calling him.

"We've got some news!" he said.

Matt came slowly down the stairs. Sam was jumping up and down with excitement and Dad – well, Dad looked like he had in the old days, before Mum died.

"What – what's happened?"

"Tell you when we get there," said Sam. "We're going back to my house. Mummy and Daddy want to see you both together."

Matt wondered what secret the pair were hugging to themselves. Perhaps the Coopers had organised a holiday. A cruise, or a trip to the Caribbean. He couldn't imagine why his father should be so excited – unless of course it was a trip home to the States.

Seeing the Coopers again Matt could see why Sam had not been taken in for a moment by the imposters, uncanny though the likeness had been. The real Coopers were a warm, lively, vital couple. The two actors who'd replaced them had been dull and colourless.

They both hugged Matt. "It's so good to see you again," said Mrs Cooper. "I'm sorry it's taken a few days but there were things to arrange. Now, come and have some lunch and then we can talk."

A beaming Mrs Miles, back in charge of the kitchen, brought a large tray laden with quiche and salad to a table set beneath a parasol on the terrace.

"The dining room is still out of action," said Mr Cooper ruefully. "You two certainly made a thorough job of wrecking it!"

"I'm sorry," said Matt.

"No, no, don't be sorry! It was a very effective ruse! I'd never have thought of it."

"Well, it was Sam, actually - "

"You should have seen their faces!" Sam gloated.

"Yes," said Mrs Cooper, "but – let's not think about those awful people any more. It's in the past now and we have our happy life back again."

As she was cutting up the large quiche and transferring portions to their plates, Sam leaned towards Matt. It seemed that she couldn't keep a smile off her face. "Wait till you hear!" she whispered.

"Eat first, talk later," said Mr Cooper. He raised his glass of wine. "A toast. To the future!"

"The future," echoed the others.

Matt sipped his orange juice. Did he have a future? The others were all smiling at him and he felt a prickle of something. Excitement? Hope?

"Now to business," said Mr Cooper, when Mrs Miles had removed their plates and served coffee.

"We've decided to sell this house. It's been my family's home for generations and it will be a wrench, but now there are too many bad memories." He looked at his wife and daughter. "So we've made a decision to move away from England."

So that was it. Matt wondered if, six months hence, Sam would even remember him.

"It's been in my mind for some time to find a property abroad," Mr Cooper went on. "Somewhere with a warmer, more stable climate, and with sufficient land to grow an unlimited range of plants. I also want space to build my own laboratory – and perhaps even a small training centre."

Matt stirred his coffee and waited,.

"We're thinking of California," said Mrs Cooper. "And we've asked your father to help."

Don't say anything, Matt told himself. Don't let them see you care. He picked up his cup and took a large mouthful of coffee, then found himself unable to get it past the hard lump in his throat.

"We think he has the experience we need," said Mr Cooper. "He knows the area, he can help us find the right property, and then with his project management skills he can supervise the new building."

So Dad would get his wish. To go back to the States. And Matt? Back to the Home. Nothing changed.

Maybe one day, when the Coopers' building project was finished, his Dad might spare a passing thought for him, he thought bitterly. And maybe – if he hadn't by then got caught up in a new life – maybe he'd invite him over.

But did they know about Dad's drinking? If they did, surely they wouldn't employ him, however grateful they were. Matt could stop all this in its tracks if he told them, and why shouldn't he?

He looked down at his cup, then up at his father.

"Have you – did you tell them - ?"

"They know about the drinking," said his father quickly. "And they're willing to take a chance on me. I've already stopped, Matt. I stopped as soon as I knew you'd run away and I realised what a mess I was making of my life. Our lives."

"Sometimes terrible circumstances – like your mother's sudden death, Matt – change people," said Mrs Cooper gently. "But we've every confidence that your father can make a new start, and we'll be around to help."

And me? Matt wanted to ask.

"It may take quite some time to sell this house and to find the right site in California. So we were wondering, Matt, if you'd like to come here and live with us in the meantime. There's a good school only a few miles away."

"I'm going to transfer there too," said Sam. "I don't want to board any more, and it'll probably only be for one term anyway. We can go together. Won't that be great?"

Great? Yes, he guessed it would be. But after that? No-one had said what was to happen to him after the Coopers left England.

"Excuse me," he muttered. "I need the bathroom." He

blundered to his feet, hearing the tinkle of breaking china as his coffee cup hit the terrace, and fled into the house.

"Matt! Matt!" he heard Sam calling. "Wait!"

She caught up with him at the top of the stairs.

"What's wrong? We thought you'd be excited!"

"Excited! Because you're all off to California to have a great new life? Why should I be excited?"

"But - " Sam stared at him. "Surely you didn't think – You must have realised that you'd be coming too!"

He turned his face away. "My Dad didn't say anything."

"Well, we all took it for granted you'd know. Oh Matt, how could you be so stupid? Of course we wouldn't leave you behind. You're our saviour!" Sam flung her arms around him. "Come back outside. Please."

He wanted to believe. But it was hard to forget all the broken promises of the past year, the way his Dad had abandoned him.

Sam must have read his thoughts. "You have to give him a second chance, Matt. He does love you, I'm sure of it. Come on, come and talk to him."

Outside, his father was chatting quietly to the Coopers. He looked up anxiously as Matt reappeared.

"I'm sorry, son. I should have said right away. Matt, I don't intend ever to lose you again. And I won't let you down again, I promise."

Matt looked at them all. At his father, whose eyes were moist. At the smiling Coopers. At Sam's funny, foxy face. He thought of the misery of the past year. And he thought of all that had happened in just two short weeks to change his life, to bring him and his Dad together again, to meet Sam and the Coopers, and to be given the prospect of a wonderful new life.

He had been robbed, he had been imprisoned, he had been shot at, and the memory of climbing up that chimney still made him shudder.

But had it all been worth it?

Yes!

THE END

Made in the USA
Middletown, DE
12 December 2020